Daniela could feel vibrations of evil coming from the *Comte*, as together they stood before the altar.

The Parson opened his Prayer Book.

He was half-way through the first prayer of the Marriage Service when a voice from the back of the Church said loudly:

"Stop this marriage!"

Daniela thought she must be dreaming.

She knew with a leap of her heart that the Marquis was there.

He walked up the aisle, his footsteps ringing out.

Daniela looked at him with shining eyes.

"You have... saved me! I was... quite certain... I would have... to die!"

A Camfield Novel of Love
by Barbara Cartland

———

"Barbara Cartland's novels are all distinguished by their intelligence, good sense, and good nature..."

— **ROMANTIC TIMES**

"Who could give better advice on how to keep your romance going strong than the world's most famous romance novelist, Barbara Cartland?"

— **THE STAR**

Camfield Place,
Hatfield
Hertfordshire,
England

Dearest Reader,

Camfield Novels of Love mark a very exciting era of my books with Jove. They have already published nearly two hundred of my titles since they became my first publisher in America, and now all my original paperback romances in the future will be published exclusively by them.

As you already know, Camfield Place in Hertfordshire is my home, which originally existed in 1275, but was rebuilt in 1867 by the grandfather of Beatrix Potter.

It was here in this lovely house, with the best view in the country, that she wrote *The Tale of Peter Rabbit*. Mr. McGregor's garden is exactly as she described it. The door in the wall that the fat little rabbit could not squeeze underneath and the goldfish pool where the white cat sat twitching its tail are still there.

I had Camfield Place blessed when I came here in 1950 and was so happy with my husband until he died, and now with my children and grandchildren, that I know the atmosphere is filled with love and we have all been very lucky.

It is easy here to write of love and I know you will enjoy the Camfield Novels of Love. Their plots are definitely exciting and the covers very romantic. They come to you, like all my books, with love.

Bless you,

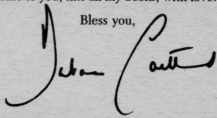

CAMFIELD NOVELS OF LOVE
by Barbara Cartland

THE POOR GOVERNESS	NEVER FORGET LOVE	RIDING IN THE SKY
WINGED VICTORY	HELGA IN HIDING	LOVERS IN LISBON
LUCKY IN LOVE	SAFE AT LAST	LOVE IS INVINCIBLE
LOVE AND THE MARQUIS	HAUNTED	THE GODDESS OF LOVE
A MIRACLE IN MUSIC	CROWNED WITH LOVE	AN ADVENTURE OF LOVE
LIGHT OF THE GODS	ESCAPE	THE HERB FOR HAPPINESS
BRIDE TO A BRIGAND	THE DEVIL DEFEATED	ONLY A DREAM
LOVE COMES WEST	THE SECRET OF THE	SAVED BY LOVE
A WITCH'S SPELL	MOSQUE	LITTLE TONGUES OF FIRE
SECRETS	A DREAM IN SPAIN	A CHIEFTAIN FINDS LOVE
THE STORMS OF LOVE	THE LOVE TRAP	THE LOVELY LIAR
MOONLIGHT ON THE SPHINX	LISTEN TO LOVE	THE PERFUME OF THE GODS
WHITE LILAC	THE GOLDEN CAGE	A KNIGHT IN PARIS
REVENGE OF THE HEART	LOVE CASTS OUT FEAR	REVENGE IS SWEET
THE ISLAND OF LOVE	A WORLD OF LOVE	THE PASSIONATE PRINCESS
THERESA AND A TIGER	DANCING ON A RAINBOW	SOLITA AND THE SPIES
LOVE IS HEAVEN	LOVE JOINS THE CLANS	THE PERFECT PEARL
MIRACLE FOR A MADONNA	AN ANGEL RUNS AWAY	LOVE IS A MAZE
A VERY UNUSUAL WIFE	FORCED TO MARRY	A CIRCUS FOR LOVE
THE PERIL AND THE PRINCE	BEWILDERED IN BERLIN	THE TEMPLE OF LOVE
ALONE AND AFRAID	WANTED—A WEDDING RING	THE BARGAIN BRIDE
TEMPTATION OF A TEACHER	THE EARL ESCAPES	THE HAUNTED HEART
ROYAL PUNISHMENT	STARLIGHT OVER TUNIS	REAL LOVE OR FAKE
THE DEVILISH DECEPTION	THE LOVE PUZZLE	KISS FROM A STRANGER
PARADISE FOUND	LOVE AND KISSES	A VERY SPECIAL LOVE
LOVE IS A GAMBLE	SAPPHIRES IN SIAM	THE NECKLACE OF LOVE
A VICTORY FOR LOVE	A CARETAKER OF LOVE	A REVOLUTION OF LOVE
LOOK WITH LOVE	SECRETS OF THE HEART	THE MARQUIS WINS

Other Books by Barbara Cartland

THE ADVENTURER	THE IRRESISTIBLE BUCK	OPEN WINGS
AGAIN THIS RAPTURE	THE KISS OF PARIS	A RAINBOW TO HEAVEN
BARBARA CARTLAND'S	THE KISS OF THE DEVIL	THE RELUCTANT BRIDE
BOOK OF BEAUTY AND	A KISS OF SILK	THE SCANDALOUS LIFE OF
HEALTH	THE KNAVE OF HEARTS	KING CAROL
BLUE HEATHER	THE LEAPING FLAME	THE SECRET FEAR
BROKEN BARRIERS	A LIGHT TO THE HEART	THE SMUGGLED HEART
THE CAPTIVE HEART	LIGHTS OF LOVE	A SONG OF LOVE
THE COIN OF LOVE	THE LITTLE PRETENDER	STARS IN MY HEART
THE COMPLACENT WIFE	LOST ENCHANTMENT	STOLEN HALO
COUNT THE STARS	LOVE AT FORTY	SWEET ENCHANTRESS
DESIRE OF THE HEART	LOVE FORBIDDEN	SWEET PUNISHMENT
DESPERATE DEFIANCE	LOVE IN HIDING	THEFT OF A HEART
THE DREAM WITHIN	LOVE IS THE ENEMY	THE THIEF OF LOVE
ELIZABETHAN LOVER	LOVE ME FOREVER	THIS TIME IT'S LOVE
THE ENCHANTING EVIL	LOVE TO THE RESCUE	TOUCH A STAR
ESCAPE FROM PASSION	LOVE UNDER FIRE	TOWARDS THE STARS
FOR ALL ETERNITY	THE MAGIC OF HONEY	THE UNKNOWN HEART
A GOLDEN GONDOLA	METTERNICH THE	WE DANCED ALL
A HAZARD OF HEARTS	PASSIONATE DIPLOMAT	NIGHT
A HEART IS BROKEN	MONEY, MAGIC AND	THE WINGS OF ECSTASY
THE HIDDEN HEART	MARRIAGE	THE WINGS OF LOVE
THE HORIZONS OF LOVE	NO HEART IS FREE	WINGS ON MY HEART
IN THE ARMS OF LOVE	THE ODIOUS DUKE	WOMAN, THE ENIGMA

A NEW CAMFIELD NOVEL OF LOVE BY

BARBARA CARTLAND

The Marquis Wins

AUG 07 1990

J

JOVE BOOKS, NEW YORK

THE MARQUIS WINS

A Jove Book / published by arrangement with
the author

PRINTING HISTORY
Jove edition / July 1990

ISBN: 0-515-10355-1

Jove Books are published by The Berkley Publishing Group,
200 Madison Avenue, New York, New York 10016.
The name "JOVE" and the "J" logo
are trademarks belonging to Jove Publications, Inc.

PRINTED IN THE UNITED STATES OF AMERICA

10 9 8 7 6 5 4 3 2 1

Author's Note

I visited Baden-Baden first in 1933 and thought it one of the most beautiful places I had ever seen.

Now, when I have travelled all over the world, I still think the same.

There is something magical about the ancient town and the glorious Casino, all gold and crystal.

The gardens slope down from the Fairytale Bremer Park Hotel to the slow-moving River Oos with its tinkling cascades and romantic bridges.

In *A Gamble with Hearts,* my first novel set in Baden-Baden, and my second *The Marquis Wins,* the Heroine stays in the Stephanie Hotel which was named by the Grand Duchess Stephanie, who in 1806 made Baden-Baden famous.

A niece of the Empress Josephine, it was Napoleon

who married her to the Grand Duke Karl Frederick of Baden.

Unhappy in the marriage, Stephanie made Baden-Baden the centre of her life, and as the elite of Europe were entertained in her Salon, the town became known as "Stephanie's Capital."

The Stephanie Hotel soon became too small to accommodate so many visitors.

Today, it has become the Bremer Park, but one can feel the glamour and beauty which the lovely Duchess left behind.

She still touches the hearts of all who stay in Baden-Baden.

The Marquis Wins

chapter one

1867

"Faites vos jeux, Messieurs, Mesdames."

There was a quick movement round the Roulette Table to put on the chips, many of which were to the value of two thousand francs.

There was then the usual anxious silence until the Croupier's voice rang out:

"Vingt-neuf—noir, impair et passe."

There was a little gasp, for the Marquis of Crowle had won again.

The huge pile of chips on *vingt-neuf* increased.

As the Croupier pushed it towards him, its progress was watched with envy and greed.

The Marquis, his face impressive and cynical, collected his winnings and rose to his feet.

"You are leaving, *Monsieur*?" a very attractive Frenchwoman asked, who had been sitting beside him.

"I never push my luck," the Marquis replied in a bored voice.

He walked away from the table and changed his winnings, which were considerable, into bank notes.

He was deciding what he should do next.

It had certainly been an auspicious day so far.

His horse had won at the races, and he had certainly won the cost of coming to Baden-Baden just now at the tables.

Actually he had come on an impulse.

Having bought two outstanding horses in Paris, he had, after amusing himself there with one of the most notorious Courtesans, intended to return to England.

She informed him that she was going to Baden-Baden.

He thought he would like to try out his horses first on the Continent before they joined his outstanding stable at Newmarket.

Cora Pearl had obviously believed his sole reason for coming to Baden-Baden was to follow her.

One of the most successful and certainly one of the most exotic of the great Courtesans of Paris, she was in fact English.

She had been born Eliza Emma Crouch, the daughter of a Plymouth Music-Teacher.

She had been seduced by a middle-aged diamond merchant when she was only twenty.

Spirited, with an exquisite figure and glossy red hair, she had been taken by the merchant to a drinking-den near Covent Garden.

After she had accepted the drink he had offered her, she found herself recovering from unconsciousness beside him in bed.

This experience had left her with a hatred for men which remained with her for the rest of her life.

She held them spellbound, fleeced them, used them, hurt them, and invariably left them.

She never felt tenderness or love for any man.

It was because of this unusual twist to her character that she had attracted the Marquis.

He felt very much the same about women as she did about men.

Because of his indifference, and also because he was exceedingly rich, handsome, and a success at everything he undertook, women never left him alone.

He would in fact have found it surprising to meet an attractive woman who did not attempt to capture him.

In the Social World this would have been a recognised feather in her cap.

The same applied to the other world of the *Demi-Monde*, both in England and in France.

However fair the Charmer, however hard she tried, the Marquis was inevitably bored after a very short time.

Despite her pleas and however many tears she shed, he left her.

Cora's tough attitude to life amused him.

It was perhaps her piquancy, her English accent, her ruthlessness, and her outrageous behaviour that proved as seductive as her perfect figure.

She had begun what she called her "Golden Chain of Lovers" with a Duke and a Prince.

She added the Prince of Orange, heir to the throne of the Netherlands.

The most intelligent, distinguished, and gifted of her lovers, however, was the *Duc* de Morny, half-brother of the Emperor of France.

The *Duc* had all the qualities that Cora Pearl respected—toughness, intelligence, wealth, extravagance, and rank.

He also occasionally showed her what she found an endearing loyalty.

Once, when she had been turned away from the Casino at Baden-Baden, he offered her his arm.

She entered the Casino in triumph, escorted by the son of Queen Hortense.

The *Duc* was now dead, and she had embarked on an affair with the Prince Napoleon, who was renowned for his many notorious liaisons.

They were certainly two of a pair. Cora Pearl had said to her friends:

"The man is an angel to those who please him, but profligate, unmanageable, insolent, and a devil to everyone else."

Because much the same could be applied to the Marquis, it was not surprising that he and Cora should have found much in common.

She was one of the sights of Paris that the Marquis found difficult to ignore.

She had reached her dazzling zenith and was so rich that her jewels were worth a million francs.

She gave stupendous entertainments, grand dinners, masked Balls, impromptu suppers.

At the suppers the peaches and grapes did not rest on the customary vine-leaves but on fifteen-hundred francs' worth of Parma violets.

She had come to Baden-Baden without the Prince Napoleon, but she was never content with only one lover.

Victor Masséna, third *Duc* de Rivoli was her protector.

He paid her chef, Salé, who sometimes spent thirty thousand francs on food in a fortnight, and he gave her money to lose at the Baden Casino.

He was furious when he found Cora was giving her money to the young Prince Achille Murat.

Masséna had given Cora her first horse and she rode like an Amazon.

She was known as being kinder to her horses than to her lovers.

She had, the Marquis discovered, bought sixty superb saddle and carriage horses and in the last three years spent ninety thousand francs with one horse-dealer alone.

On one thing he was determined.

He would not give Cora his French horse, which had today carried his colours first past the winning-post.

A few years earlier visitors to Baden-Baden had been surprised to find a new Théâtre, made from two-coloured sandstone, had been built.

It was the creation of the Parisian Architect, Derchy.

It was a huge success from the moment it opened, and Cora could not resist an invitation to appear on the stage.

She had as Cupid created a sensation in Paris at the Théâtre les Bouffes-Parisiens.

A Count had offered fifty thousand francs for the boots in which Cora ran on stage.

"I remember very little of the performance," one of the Marquis's friends had said to him when he arrived in Paris, "except that Cora Pearl plays Cupid with great self-possession. She wears very few garments, but the buttons of her boots are large diamonds of the purest water."

The Marquis had laughed.

"I have already been told," he said, "that in one last extravagant gambol she throws herself on her back and flings

5

her legs up in the air to show that the soles of her shoes are one mass of diamonds!''

After that it was obvious that Cora Pearl would be amused when the Marquis, on meeting her, presented her with a box of Marrons-glacés.

Each Marron was separately wrapped in a thousand-franc note.

As the Marquis moved through the crowd round the Roulette Tables, several attractive women greeted him and put a restraining hand on his arm, hoping to hold his attention.

He passed them by with a look of indifference.

The disdain on his face was so characteristic that few people, having seen him once or twice, bothered to comment on it.

The Casino in Baden-Baden was not only the oldest Casino in Germany, but indisputably the most beautiful.

The walls of the Salle Louis-Quatorze with its exquisitely painted ceiling and huge chandeliers was unique.

But it was rivalled by the Louis Treize Hall with its delightful murals.

The whole Casino had an atmosphere that was different from any other the Marquis had ever visited.

He thought also that the company was more distinguished and the women lovelier than he remembered anywhere else.

But it was a hot evening, and for the moment, as he had no more desire to play, he needed air.

He stepped out into the garden at the back of the Casino.

There were fairy-lights along the paths, and Chinese lanterns in the trees.

It had a magical appearance that was somehow part of the stars overhead, and a new moon was rising over the mountains.

There were only a few people in the garden, for who

could resist the tables, where fortunes were changing hands?

Besides, there was the sight not only of the great aristocrats of Europe but of a number of the most beautiful and most notorious Courtesans from Paris.

The *Duc* de Joinville was at the side of the beautiful Madeleine Brohan, the star of the *Comédie Française*.

The Light Opera Diva, Hortense Schneider, had come in from the stage of the Casino Théâtre.

The Marquis, however, walked alone into the garden and felt the soft clear air was a relief.

He was not thinking of women, but of the way his horse had passed the winning-post a length in front of the other runners.

This was to the fury of several French owners who had been confident of winning the very large prizes that had been offered to tempt the best horses in Europe to Baden-Baden.

The Valley of Oos was not spacious enough for the fabled Sport of Kings.

Jacques Dupressoir, the organiser of the Casino Hunts, had found the most splendid location near the village of Iffezheim.

The Parisian Jockey Club had taken over the direction of what was to be a Badenian Longchamps.

It had cost the lessee of the Casino, Edouard Benazet, three hundred thousand francs for the track and the three spectator stands.

He had found that as an investment it was worth every sou.

The Marquis was thinking it was a great achievement to have beaten the French owners.

He thought it would be even more satisfactory if tomorrow he could win the principal race.

He supposed that Cora would expect most, if not all, of his winning to be spent on her.

He wondered somewhat cynically what he could give her that she had not already got.

He had learnt in Paris that actual money meant little or nothing to her.

She was by now a wealthy woman and Prince Napoleon was extremely generous.

He gave her twelve-thousand francs a month and she regularly spent twice as much.

She owned two or three houses, furnished quite regardless of expense.

It was difficult to know what sort of present would be original and different from what she had received from anyone else.

The Marquis knew, because she was so unpredictable, that if she was not pleased with what she was given, she would not hesitate to refuse it.

Prince Paul Demidoff, a Russian of untold wealth, had insisted just to annoy her on wearing his hat at the Restaurant Maison d'Or.

Cora had smashed his cane over his head, an incident which she told the Marquis she regretted because the cane was a good one.

When the Prince in revenge claimed her pearls were not real, she threw her necklace on the floor, where it broke and the pearls rolled away in all directions.

"Pick up the pearls, my dear," she said scathingly. "I will prove they are real and give you one for your cravat."

The Prince sat transfixed, but the nobility who were dining at the Maison d'Or went down on their hands and knees to salvage the pearls.

The Marquis had laughed at the story.

He remembered that four years earlier Cora had fought a duel in the Bois de Boulogne with another Courtesan, Marthe de Vère.

They were quarrelling over a handsome Armenian Prince.

Both women had used their riding-whips freely and slashed each other's faces.

They did not appear in public for the following week, during which time their Adonis vanished and all Paris had laughed uproariously.

"Now, what can I give her?" the Marquis asked himself.

Then unexpectedly he decided that it was too much trouble.

Making one of his characteristic quick decisions which invariably stunned his friends, he decided that immediately after the races he would return to England.

He did not suppose Cora would mind, nor did it matter to him if she did.

For no apparent reason, and he had no intention of trying to find one, he had had enough.

He would go back to Crowle Hall, where there were a dozen matters awaiting his attention.

He was quite certain, too, there would be a huge number of invitations from London requesting his presence.

"I will go home," he decided.

There would be no regrets for anything he might leave behind.

It was then that a small, soft, nervous little voice said beside him:

"M-may I . . . speak to you . . . My Lord?"

He looked up from where he was sitting and saw in the light from one of the Chinese lanterns above him that a young girl was standing at his side.

She was small, slender, and he saw two very large eyes that seemed to fill her pointed face.

She was speaking in English.

He was sure she had just seen him win a good deal of money and was going to petition him.

It was something that constantly happened in a Casino.

Usually the women offered themselves in exchange and were surprised when he refused.

Because he did not answer the girl said:

"I . . . I know it is . . . incorrect for me to . . . bother you . . . but I . . . I am . . . desperate. I can only . . . beg of you . . . because you are English . . . to help me."

"I presume by that," the Marquis replied in a disdainful tone, "that you require some money!"

"N-no . . . My Lord . . . I want something . . . very different."

This was certainly a surprise.

Then the Marquis, almost against his better judgement, said:

"I suggest you sit down beside me and explain yourself."

He saw the girl give a glance over her shoulder towards the lights of the Casino before she moved past him to sit down.

She did not, as he had expected she would, sit near to him, but as far away as it was possible to be.

Now she was facing the lights of the Gaming Room and the Marquis could see she was very young and, unless he was mistaken, very lovely.

She had fair hair which seemed to glitter as if it were touched by the stars.

She had huge eyes and a small, straight nose, beneath which her perfectly shaped lips were, he thought, trembling a little with fear.

Because she was so obviously upset he said in a kinder voice than he generally used:

"Now, what is worrying you? Perhaps first you should tell me who you are."

"My name . . . is . . . Daniela Brooke," she replied.

"Brooke?" the Marquis murmured almost to himself, thinking he knew a number of Brookes.

"My father was . . . Lord Seabrooke and I have heard him speak of you . . . and your horses."

"I remember meeting your father at Newmarket," the Marquis said, "but that was some time ago."

"Papa is . . . d-dead," the girl said, "and that is why I am asking . . . you for your . . . help."

"In what way?"

"Could you . . . possibly . . . help me to . . . escape back to . . . England?"

The Marquis looked at her in surprise.

"Escape?" he questioned. "What do you mean by that?"

Daniela looked at the Casino.

"Please," she begged, "listen to . . . me . . . but . . . could we go a little farther away . . . if they . . . look for me . . . I shall have to . . . go with them . . . and I may not . . . get the chance to . . . speak to you again."

Again the Marquis made one of his quick decisions.

Instead of arguing or asking any more questions, he rose to his feet.

"I am sure we shall find another seat a little farther from the lights, where we will not be disturbed."

Daniela rose with the grace of a young fawn.

They moved over the soft grass until the lights of the Casino were almost out of sight.

Then, as the Marquis expected, they found another seat

11

conveniently placed under a tree and flanked by concealing shrubs.

It was a place made for lovers, but he noticed that Daniela sat, as she had before, at the far end of the seat.

Crossing his legs, he asked:

"Now, what is all this about, and when did your father die?"

"Four . . . weeks ago."

The Marquis stared at Daniela in astonishment.

"Four weeks ago, and you are here at Baden-Baden?"

"That . . . is what I want to . . . explain to you."

"I am listening."

He thought as he spoke that this was certainly an unusual encounter in the Casino, of all places.

Despite himself, he was curious as to what he was about to hear.

Daniela told her story in a very low voice.

As she unravelled her remarkable tale, the Marquis, listening, realised that she was not only well-educated, but also intelligent.

She told him first how her mother had decided she should complete her education at a Convent Finishing School in St. Cloud just outside Paris.

Lady Seabrooke had been anxious, Daniela explained, that her daughter should speak languages fluently, especially French.

"The world is growing smaller," she had told her, "and people travel far more than they used to. So many of the English find themselves unable to communicate with anyone in a foreign country and just shout louder!"

She had smiled and went on:

"That is why, my dearest, I want you to become proficient both in French and Italian, and, although it is an ugly language, to learn a little German."

"I was happy at the School in St. Cloud," Daniela said. "The Nuns were very kind to us, and we had the best teachers procurable anywhere in Paris."

The Marquis learned that a year ago quite unexpectedly her mother had died.

It had happened so quickly that it was hard for Daniela to realise she had lost someone she adored, and her father was distraught.

"I went back to England and stayed with Papa," she told the Marquis, "but after I had been there for two months he insisted I should finish my studies. I therefore went back to France."

The Marquis was listening and wondering how this could possibly concern him.

He found that Daniela's soft, musical voice had an almost hypnotic quality about it.

He was therefore far more interested than he usually was in other people's troubles.

"After I left England," Daniela said, "Papa came to Paris. He told me later that he had found our home so empty without Mama that he felt he could . . . not bear it . . . any more. He rented a house in the Rue du Faubourg St. Honoré."

She paused before she added:

"It was very exciting to know he was near me, but after he had been in Paris for . . . a month or so I became a . . . little worried."

There was silence for a moment, as if she were trying to choose her words carefully.

"Why?" the Marquis asked.

"I felt," Daniela replied, "that Papa, who had always lived a . . . quiet life as a Country Gentleman, was becom-

ing . . . involved in the . . . gaieties of Paris of which . . .
Mama would not . . . have approved.''

"How could you know anything about them?" the Marquis asked somewhat cynically.

"The girls at School had brothers who told them how much they . . . enjoyed the Théâtres and the Restaurants. They also talked about the . . . beautiful ladies who were not . . . accepted in their . . . homes.''

The Marquis saw as she spoke that Daniela's eyes flickered and she looked away from him.

He thought, too, that the colour rose in her cheeks.

He knew only too well exactly what she was implying.

He was doubtful if she had any idea of the exotic behaviour of women like Cora Pearl and the other famous Courtesans.

But suspected stories of their fantastic appearance and extravagance had in some way percolated into her School.

"When I saw Papa," Daniela went on, "which was usually about . . . once a week . . . he began to look . . . tired and . . . different from how he had been when he was . . . at home in the country with our dogs, horses, and, of course . . . Mama."

There was a little sob in her voice.

The Marquis realised it was only with a tremendous effort at self-control that she was able to go on:

"Then one day . . . when I was having . . . luncheon with Papa a . . . Lady arrived."

As she spoke she was seeing again the door of the Dining-Room open and *Madame* Esmé Blanc come into the room.

She was not a pretty woman.

At the same time, Daniela had never seen anyone so smart in what she thought was a slightly over-dressed, exaggerated manner, but undoubtedly what the French would call *chic*.

She was not young, and her face was rouged and powdered while her lips were very red.

As she stared at the newcomer, Daniela was aware that her father had stiffened and there was a frown between his eyes as he asked:

"What do you want, Esmé? I told you my daughter would be with me today."

"I know that, Arthur," *Madame* Blanc replied, "but I forgot my purse, and as I needed money, I was obliged to come back for it."

Daniela stared in astonishment.

No one had mentioned to her that there was anybody staying in the house with her father.

She had imagined he was living there alone.

Madame Blanc approached the Dining-Room table and stared at her in what she felt was an uncomfortable manner.

"So this is your daughter about whom I have heard so much!" she exclaimed. "I am very delighted—no, enchanted—to meet her."

She spoke English with a slight accent and her last words were deliberately gushing.

Daniela knew what she said was completely insincere: she was not delighted to meet her, but was, in fact, antagonistic.

She had risen from her chair to hold out her hand.

"How do you do, *Madame*," she said because she thought it was polite.

Madame Blanc had merely touched her hand with gloved fingers.

"Now that I have seen you, I understand why your dear father, who is such a kind person, is so devoted to you," she said.

Lord Seabrooke had not moved, but only sat frowning,

obviously disconcerted by *Madame* Blanc's appearance.

Now, in a voice of authority that Daniela recognised, he said:

"That is enough, Esmé! You have satisfied your curiosity and I am sure you have other things to do."

"But of course, *mon cher*," *Madame* Blanc replied, "and if I have annoyed you, I will apologise later this evening."

She smiled at Lord Seabrooke in what Daniela thought was a somewhat familiar manner.

Turning with a flounce of her skirts, she swept from the room, leaving behind her an uncomfortable atmosphere and the scent of a very exotic French perfume.

As Daniela sat down again her father said:

"I should have told you that *Madame* Blanc is staying here for a few nights."

"Who is she, Papa?" Daniela asked. "I have not heard you speak of her."

"No," Lord Seabrooke admitted vaguely. "I met her at a dinner party, and she asked if she could be my guest."

Daniela was aware the next week when she came out to luncheon with him again that *Madame* Blanc was still in the house.

She found out quite by accident that the door of the bedroom next her father's was locked and thought it strange.

There was a pair of woman's gloves on the hall table beside those her father wore.

There was a sunshade amongst the umbrellas.

She was aware, too, of an exotic perfume lingering on the cushions in the Salon and in the passage out of which the locked room opened.

She found herself thinking about *Madame* Blanc and wondering how her father could find her interesting after he had been so happy and content with her mother.

Their home had always seemed to be filled with laughter.

She had seen him at her mother's funeral, hollow-eyed and pale like a man stricken by a mortal blow.

It seemed extraordinary that he should have found consolation, if that was the right word for it, so quickly.

Then in the middle of the week she was told by one of the Nuns that her father had arrived at the Convent and wanted to speak to her.

She had gone hastily to the Mother Superior's room to find him there looking, she thought, rather strange.

"What is it, Papa? What is the . . . matter?" she asked.

Then, as he did not answer, she asked:

"You are not . . . going back to . . . England?"

"No, not at the moment," he said, "but there is something I have to tell you."

She waited, but he was looking round the small Sitting-Room with its Crucifix on the wall and a *prie-dieu* in front of it.

"I cannot talk to you here," he said. "I have asked the Mother Superior if I can take you out to luncheon, and she has agreed."

Daniela's eyes lit up.

"Oh, Papa, how exciting! I shall feel I am playing truant, but it will be thrilling to be with you!"

"Hurry and put on your bonnet!" her father said sharply.

She ran off to obey him, but she knew as she stepped into his carriage, which was waiting outside, that there was something very wrong.

She thought then for the first time that she ought never to have left her father alone.

When her mother had died, however much he might have

protested, she should have stayed with him in England.

Afterwards, when she looked back, it seemed to Daniela that she grew up at that moment.

She ceased to be a child, doing whatever the grown-ups decreed, and began to think for herself.

She had slipped her hand into her father's.

"Do not look so worried, Papa," she said.

"I am here, and if you are going back to England, I will come with you and look after you as Mama would have done if she were alive."

Her father's fingers tightened so that she almost cried out at the pain of it.

Then he said in a strange voice:

"For God's sake, Daniela, do not talk like that!"

She was somewhat startled and remained silent until the carriage drew up outside a small, quiet Restaurant.

It was comfortable and expensive, with only two other tables occupied.

On her father's insistence, they were given a table in an alcove which was almost like being alone in a small room.

Her father studied the menu.

As he did so, Daniela watched him and saw he was looking pale and drawn.

It flashed through her mind that perhaps he was ill.

Quite suddenly she felt afraid.

When he had given their order and the waiter had withdrawn, she put out her hand to her father, saying:

"Please, Papa . . . tell me what has . . . upset you."

Then Lord Seabrooke, in a voice that did not sound like his own, said heavily:

"I do not know . . . how to tell you this, Daniela, but . . . I am married!"

"M-married?" Daniela exclaimed.

Whatever else she had expected, it had certainly not been this.

"I . . . I do not understand . . ."

Her father was silent. Then he said:

"Nor do I, but it happened when I did not know what I was . . . doing."

Daniela stared at him and he said:

"Esmé Blanc, whom you met although I expressly told her not to come near us, was determined from the start to marry me because I am a rich man."

Daniela made a little murmur of horror, but she did not interrupt and her father went on:

"She begged me, pleaded with me, but I was adamant that no one, and I meant no one, should ever take your mother's place."

There was an agony in her father's voice as he spoke of her mother that made the tears come into Daniela's eyes.

"Besides that," Lord Seabrooke continued, "I had no intention of giving you a stepmother, least of all a woman like Esmé Blanc!"

Daniela looked at him in astonishment.

"But she is a friend of yours, Papa! You had her to stay."

Lord Seabrooke drew in his breath.

"I was lonely, dearest, as you can understand. The reason why I came to France was that I could not bear the emptiness of the rooms at home and expecting any minute the door to open and your mother to come in."

"I do understand that," Daniela said, "and I should have stayed with you."

"It is too late now," Lord Seabrooke said. "This woman has got her way and, although I can hardly believe it myself, she is my wife!"

"But . . . how could you have . . . asked her to . . . marry you?" Daniela asked.

"I swear to you, and you know I always tell you the truth, I did not ask her to marry me. I had no intention of marrying her, and she is not a woman I would inflict on you as a stepmother!"

He spoke so violently that Daniela looked at him again in astonishment.

"Then how . . . how did it . . . happen?"

"I do not remember anything about it," Lord Seabrooke said. "We had dinner and some of her friends were there— none of whom I would introduce to you. After the dinner was over I remember nothing!"

"Nothing?" Daniela questioned.

"Nothing until I woke up in bed the next morning and was shown the Marriage Lines, signed by the Parson who married us at a small Church in Montmartre."

"It is . . . legal?" Daniela asked.

"Esmé Blanc had arranged the formalities which must take place in France at the *Mairie*. A friend of hers impersonated me and signed my name."

"B-but . . . Papa . . . !"

Daniela could only exclaim in horror at what she had just heard.

After a moment she said, as her father did not speak:

"But surely . . . Papa . . . in those . . . circumstances, it must be . . . illegal?"

"I would have to prove it in the French Courts," Lord Seabrooke replied. "It would be a long-drawn-out case, and the details would be reported in every newspaper both here and in England!"

Daniela drew in her breath.

She knew how the scandal would hurt and humiliate her father.

She knew without his telling her how appalling it would be for him to have to admit that he had allowed a woman like Esmé Blanc to stay with him in his house.

And anyhow, because he was English, he might not win his case.

There was a long pause before she said in a whisper:

"What are . . . you going to . . . do about it, Papa?"

"I do not know," Lord Seabrooke replied, "but I wanted you, my precious daughter, to know the truth."

As Daniela repeated to the Marquis his last words, she was almost choked to tears.

As if she were ashamed of her lack of control, she looked away from him.

After a moment without speaking he passed her his fine linen handkerchief.

She took it and wiped her eyes.

As she did so the Marquis thought that never in his life had he heard such an extraordinary and at the same time intriguing tale.

Because of the way she told it he could almost see the drama of it unfolding in front of his eyes.

He knew he wanted to hear what had happened after that.

He found himself hoping, which was unlike his usual indifference to anything that occurred, that they would not be interrupted.

Daniela, having wiped her eyes, sat with his handkerchief between her fingers, looking into the darkness.

"What happened next?" the Marquis asked.

There was a long silence before Daniela replied:

"Papa . . . was killed in a . . . d-duel!"

chapter two

"A duel?" the Marquis exclaimed.

He was thinking as he spoke that it was the last thing he would have expected of Lord Seabrooke.

He remembered as Daniela was talking that he had met her father once in the Jockey Club at Newmarket.

On another occasion it had been at Whites in London.

He had seemed a quiet, middle-aged man, good-looking and with a presence which, as Daniela had described it, was that of a Country Gentleman.

Duels were forbidden in England, but took place secretly.

They were more common in France, usually between the extravagant, rather flamboyant young Frenchmen who were over-emotional about their mistresses.

The Marquis would never have debased himself by being involved in one of these duels.

They occurred at a certain spot in the *Bois*, and were continually lampooned in the French Press.

Because he realised Daniela was looking depressed, he said quietly:

"Tell me what happened."

"I do not . . . know . . . exactly," she replied, "but I am sure it was . . . something to do . . . with *Madame* Blanc."

She gave a little sob before she went on:

"Whatever the reason, Papa's opponent was . . . a man who is . . . notorious for having . . . fought dozens of . . . duels, and always being . . . victorious."

"And your father was killed!" the Marquis exclaimed.

This was something which very rarely happened.

Usually the worst any man could expect from fighting in a duel was a bullet through the arm which might result in his running a high temperature.

He would also have to wear his arm in a sling for the next two or three weeks.

"It took me . . . some time," Daniela was saying in a very low voice, "to find out what . . . occurred. Finally I learnt that Papa's valet, who was devoted to him, had been present."

She gave another sob as she went on:

"When the Referee called out 'Ten!' the duellers turned, Papa fired . . . into the air, and at the . . . same time . . . faced his . . . opponent."

The Marquis stared at her in astonishment.

If that had been a deliberate gesture, then Lord Seabrooke had meant to die.

"The . . . bullet," Daniela continued, "entered Papa's . . . chest near . . . the heart and when he was . . . taken back to the house . . . he . . . he died that . . . night."

It was almost impossible for her to say the words, but she managed it.

Then with what the Marquis thought was admirable courage she wiped her eyes and without waiting for him to speak said:

"When I was . . . told what . . . had happened . . . I found it . . . hard to . . . believe that Papa had . . . really left . . . me."

"I can understand that," the Marquis said.

"The Mother Superior . . . herself took me . . . into Paris, and I knew when she . . . met my . . . stepmother that she . . . disapproved of her."

The Marquis thought this was not surprising, but he did not say so.

"Did you stay in the house, or were you taken back to your School?" he asked.

"I wanted to stay with Papa . . . and pray that he . . . would now be with . . . Mama," Daniela said simply, "but my stepmother . . . insisted that I should go . . . back with . . . the Mother Superior."

The Marquis thought that was the first sensible thing he had heard about *Madame* Blanc.

Then he asked:

"But I imagine . . . your father was . . . buried in England? Why did you not . . . return there . . . for the Funeral?"

"That is just what I am . . . going to . . . explain," Daniela replied. "It was . . . of course what I . . . intended to do . . . but before arrangements were made, my stepmother sent a message to the Convent to say that I was to . . . come to Paris . . . as Papa's Solicitors were . . . arriving from . . . England."

As she went on talking, the Marquis was aware that in

her mind she could see it all happening again.

The Mother Superior had hastily bought her a black gown.

She had been driven to the house in the Rue du Faubourg St. Honoré accompanied by Sister Teresa, one of the Senior Nuns.

When she arrived she had been greeted by her stepmother, dressed in black, but in a very different style from what she was wearing herself.

Esmé Seabrooke's gown had obviously been made by one of the great French Couturiers, and was not only extremely elegant but gave no impression of mourning.

With her face made up as it had been when Daniela had first seen her, and wearing a profusion of jewels, she looked more like an actress than a widow.

She dismissed Sister Teresa in what Daniela thought was a rather rude fashion into one of the small Sitting-Rooms and took her stepdaughter into the Salon.

"Now, listen, Daniela," she said. "I have arranged for your father's Solicitors, who arrived in Paris last night, to come here today to inform us of the contents of his Will."

"You must not be surprised," her stepmother continued, "that immediately after we were married I saw to it that you father made a new Will, with generous provision for me as his wife."

Daniela lifted her chin.

"I am sure," she said quietly, "Papa will have done what is right and just."

"He certainly had to be just to me!" her stepmother said sharply. "After all, a man has to provide for his wife, and I told your father exactly what I expected."

She spoke in a hard voice.

Daniela knew without being told that her stepmother was

resenting that as her father's child she should have any of his money and wanted it all for herself.

A terrifying question came to her mind.

Had this woman persuaded her father to make a Will in which she was excluded?

Had this woman who had married him when he was under the influence of a drug, deliberately been instrumental in involving him in a duel in which he had died?

Daniela was intelligent enough to be sure that was the explanation, or something very near it.

But as it was something she could not prove, there was no point in making a scene.

She could only pray that her father had left her enough money so that she would not be beholden to her stepmother.

She had already decided and had talked it over with the Mother Superior, that she would return to England at the end of the term to be with her relations.

In fact, the Mother Superior had said:

"If, when you go over for the Funeral, dear child, they ask you to stay, I think it would be best if you did not come back."

Daniela looked slightly surprised, and the Mother Superior had gone on:

"I know that your grandfather and grandmother are alive, and I am certain if you talk to your grandmother that she will think it best for you to be at home with your own people."

Daniela was then aware that the Mother Superior was saying this because she disapproved so strongly of her stepmother.

In fact, she thought it would be a mistake for her to have any contact with Lady Seabrooke, as she might do if she was still at School.

"I will certainly talk it over with Grandmama when I get to England, Reverend Mother," she replied, "and I suppose Papa's Funeral will take place in a few days' time."

"I am sure His Lordship's Solicitors will arrange everything, and you can put yourself in their hands," the Mother Superior answered.

As she was driven to Paris, Daniela was hoping that her stepmother would make some excuse not to come to England.

She was well aware how shocked her relatives would be if they saw her.

She could not bear to think of their astonishment that her father should have married anyone who was so obviously the exact opposite to everything her mother had been.

Yet it was quite clear from the way her stepmother had just spoken to her in the Salon that she intended to grasp every penny she could of her father's fortune.

Daniela could only pray she would not be successful.

When the English Solicitors arrived, both elderly men, Daniela remembered meeting them before.

They greeted her respectfully and looked, she thought, with surprise at her stepmother.

"It is with the deepest regret," Mr. Meadowfield said to Daniela, "that I learned of your father's death, and I can only extend to you my most sincere condolences, and also those of my partner."

"Thank . . . you," Daniela murmured.

"I have asked you here this morning," Lady Seabrooke interrupted, "not only to arrange for my husband's body to be taken back to England to be buried in the family vault, but also so that I can learn the contents of his Will."

"I have already seen *Monsieur* Descourt, My Lady," Mr. Meadowfield replied, "and he should be here at any moment. As you already know, His Lordship had his last Will and Testament drawn up by *Monsieur* Descourt, who represents my firm in Paris.''

''I am aware of that,'' Lady Seabrooke said sharply, ''and *Monsieur* Descourt has also told me that my husband is to be buried in England and not, as would have been much more convenient, in Paris.''

The way she spoke told Daniela that her stepmother had already visited *Monsieur* Descourt with the intention of finding out the terms of her father's Will.

She would not otherwise have been aware that for generations the Brooke family had been buried in the Church on the estate.

There could be no question of her father's body not being taken to England.

Almost as if she were saying it aloud, Daniela was aware that Lady Seabrooke was resenting the time that she thought was being wasted by the Solicitors coming to Paris.

She also resented the delay before she could learn what was in the Will.

At that moment the door opened and a servant announced: ''*Monsieur* Descourt!''

He, too, was an elderly man, and to Daniela's relief he seemed as respectable and reliable as Mr. Meadowfield and his partner.

She had been afraid from the way her stepmother had spoken that she might have persuaded her father to go to some crooked Solicitor, a man she could bribe to change his Will after he had made it.

But Daniela knew by the cold manner in which Lady Seabrooke greeted the newcomer that he had not been persuaded to do what she wanted.

It was then Mr. Meadowfield took charge.

"I understand, My Lady, from *Monsieur* Descourt," he said coldly, "that you wish to hear the Will of your late husband. It is usual in England to wait until after the Funeral."

"That is certainly unnecessary," Lady Seabrooke replied sharply, "as the Funeral is to be in England."

"My partner and I have agreed to your request, My Lady," Mr. Meadowfield went on. "We shall take His Lordship's body back with us tomorrow, and have made all the arrangements for when we arrive in England."

"Yes, yes, I am sure you have been most competent in that respect," Lady Seabrooke said. "So now let us hear the Will which my husband made two days before he died."

She looked at Daniela as she spoke, as if she were afraid she might make some observation.

Clasping her fingers together to give her self-control, Daniela said nothing.

She was aware, however, that the Solicitors as they seated themselves were all shocked at the way her stepmother was behaving.

Mr. Meadowfield opened a brief-case which contained a number of papers.

"I have here," he said, "a copy of the Will His Lordship made before he left England."

"That is obviously invalid now!" Lady Seabrooke said sharply.

"I am aware of that, My Lady," Mr. Meadowfield replied. "At the same time, there are certain clauses which I understand from *Monsieur* Descourt are included in the new Will and would be of interest to Miss Brooke."

"I am, of course, deeply interested in anything which concerns me and my home," Daniela said.

While she was speaking to Mr. Meadowfield, *Monsieur*

Descourt had opened his brief-case and brought out a doc-ument which was obviously a Will.

He adjusted his spectacles, and then in what was good English but with a heavy accent he started to read aloud.

"The Last Will and Testament of Arthur Henry James Brooke, fifth Baron Seabrooke."

It was all in difficult, ponderous legal language which Daniela felt her stepmother might find it hard to understand.

But when *Monsieur* Descourt had finished, she gave a shrill scream.

There was no doubt that she had understood, and it was not what she had expected.

Lord Seabrooke had left his new wife a thousand pounds a year until she re-married, in which case she was to receive two hundred.

Everything else was, as in his previous Will, left in Trust to his only daughter, Daniela.

This included his house and estates in the country, a house in London, his horses at Newmarket, and everything else he possessed.

The lease of the house in Paris, which he had taken for a year, could be extended at the request of his wife, and the rent would be paid by the Solicitors.

They were, however, to be liable for nothing except the rent, and any other expenses were his wife's entire respon-sibility.

The scene her stepmother made was to Daniela both de-grading and upsetting.

Lady Seabrooke screamed at *Monsieur* Descourt, assert-ing that he had not carried out her husband's instructions.

He had been told to leave her a large capital sum of money besides a yearly allowance of ten thousand pounds.

She would, she threatened, take him to Court and accuse him of fraud.

She raged and screamed hysterically both in French and English for at least ten minutes.

Then Mr. Meadowfield in a firm tone told her there was nothing she could do but accept the thousand pounds a year.

It was, in fact, generous, as she had been married for only such a short time.

The rent of the house she was now in would be paid for as long as she wished to stay there.

"What about the bills my husband already owes?" Lady Seabrooke asked when she could speak a little more sensibly.

"Anything His Lordship owes up to the time of his death will be paid," *Monsieur* Descourt replied.

"Including my clothes and my jewels?" Lady Seabrooke enquired.

"Everything, My Lady, which is dated previous to the day on which His Lordship died."

There was a little pause before *Monsieur* Descourt added:

"I have, in fact, already been in touch with those shops I knew Your Ladyship patronised, and the bills that are unpaid are now in my possession."

Lady Seabrooke gave an audible gasp.

Daniela was aware that she had intended to produce quickly very much larger bills than those already incurred.

She would make certain they were paid for out of her husband's estate.

Daniela knew from the expressions on the faces of the three Solicitors that they had anticipated her stepmother would cheat and try to obtain every penny she could, however crooked.

"You have no right to have done that!" she screamed at

Monsieur Descourt in French and cursed him for five minutes without repeating herself.

Having been abused so rudely, he shut his brief-case and rose to his feet.

"This is quite unnecessary, *Madame*," he said, "and you will not be able to alter one word of His Lordship's Will."

The Solicitors had then taken their leave.

When they had gone, Lady Seabrooke went on screaming at the way she had been treated, abusing not only the Solicitors but her late husband as well.

Daniela was also eager to leave, and she said quietly:

"I am sorry this has happened, but you will understand that as Papa had so many obligations in England he would want me to look after the people he employed, and the house which has always been my home."

She thought she was speaking in a conciliatory manner.

Then, when her stepmother was about to rage at her again, she saw her eyes narrow as if another idea had come into her mind.

"Of course you are right, dear child," she said in a very different tone of voice, "but I am sure you will be kind and generous now that you realise how fond your father was of me, and how happy I made him."

This, Daniela knew, was a lie, but she did not wish to make things worse than they were already.

"I think what we must talk about," she said, "is the journey to England. Will you be coming with me?"

For the moment her stepmother stared at her as if it were something she had not thought about.

Then she said:

"Yes, yes, of course! How could I allow your father to be buried without my being there?"

Daniela longed to say it would be a mistake, but instead she replied:

"If we are leaving tomorrow morning, shall I send a carriage to the School to fetch my belongings? They are already packed, but I did not bring them with me in case you would not let me stay here tonight."

"Of course you must stay," Lady Seabrooke said. "There are so many things that we have to discuss, and we will have dinner quietly together. I expect we shall have to get up early to catch the train to Calais."

She then left Daniela to tell Sister Teresa what had been arranged.

The carriage had carried the Nun back to St. Cloud, to return two hours later with Daniela's luggage.

After Daniela had said goodbye to Sister Teresa, she had gone upstairs to tidy up herself for luncheon, but when she came down she found her stepmother had gone out.

It seemed a strange thing to do when she had been so insistent that she wished to talk to her.

Alone, she went to her father's room to pray by his coffin.

It had already been closed down, but there were, she found, some flowers lying on top of it, and lighted candles on each side.

She had knelt and prayed for a long time before leaving the room to find his Valet waiting for her outside.

Hudson had been with her father for many years and had known her mother. Daniela was therefore very glad to see him.

She knew the little man would be upset, and she was not surprised when there were tears in his eyes as he said:

"This be terrible, Miss Daniela—terrible! I can't 'elp thinkin' it's all a nightmare, an' we'll wake up to find th' Master's 'ere, as 'e's always been."

"I feel like that too," Daniela said. "When we get back to England we must try to do all the things he would want us to do."

"It'll never be th' same wi'out him," Hudson said pathetically, and Daniela felt the same.

They talked about England, and Daniela realised that Hudson knew more about what was happening at home than she did.

"When 'Is Lordship comes out 'ere," Hudson said, "he asked your aunt Mary to be in th' house, an' I've heard from Mrs. Field the 'Ousekeeper that everythin's just as it was when 'Er Ladyship was alive."

"That is what I hoped," Daniela murmured.

"Your aunt'll look after you 'til you gets married," Hudson remarked.

'And that will not be for a long time,' Daniela thought, although she did not say so aloud.

While her stepmother had been ranting and raving at *Monsieur* Descourt, Mr. Meadowfield had put her father's previous Will in her hand, and pointed to one particular paragraph.

She had read it and it confirmed for her in detail what *Monsieur* Descourt had just read out.

She was to receive an allowance of two thousand pounds a year until she married.

Then, when she reached twenty-five or was married, the whole of his estate would be hers.

The Solicitors, who were also the Trustees, were empowered to buy anything extra she desired, like horses, carriages, a house, or to pay for journeys outside England.

She had read it through hastily, realising that her father had been very generous to her.

She knew that her aunt Mary, her father's younger sister,

who was a widow, would doubtless be prepared to stay indefinitely in her home and chaperon her.

She was very fond of her aunt, and in a way it would be like having a little of her father with her.

She thought, too, that when she was out of mourning, either her aunt, or her grandmother, who lived in London, would present her at Court.

Because her mother would have wished it, she would take part in the Season as a rather belated *débutante*.

This was what her father had planned should happen this year when the Easter term was finished.

Even though he was married, she was sure he would have taken her back to England, but now she would be mourning for a long time.

However, she knew she would be happy with her horses.

Yet every room in the house would remind her of her father and mother and how happy they had all been together.

"I have to be sensible about this," Daniela told herself a little later in the evening.

There was still no sign of her stepmother, and she had gone again to her father's bedroom to kneel beside his coffin.

"How could . . . you have . . . left me . . . Papa?" she asked. "How could you have . . . gone away so . . . unexpectedly when there were so . . . many things we might . . . have . . . done . . . together?"

She felt the tears come into her eyes, but she fought to control them.

She had cried the whole night after she had heard that her father was dead.

Then she remembered how much he had disliked tears and scenes and, like all Englishmen, did everything to avoid them.

"You . . . must help . . . me, Mama," she said in her heart

to her mother. "I have no . . . wish to be . . . hysterical which Papa . . . would have . . . disliked, and I will . . . try to be . . . brave, although it is . . . difficult."

When she had listened to her stepmother screaming furiously at *Monsieur* Descourt, she told herself that never would she be so vulgar or so over-emotional.

At the same time, because she was alone and afraid of the future, it was difficult not to cry.

At least she could try, and try hard, to be exactly as her father would want her to be.

She went from his bedroom, and when she went downstairs she was aware that her stepmother had returned.

To her surprise, she was smiling and seemed very affable.

"I am sorry to have left you, dearest child," she said, "but there were certain people I had to see, and on the way back I called in at *Monsieur* Descourt's office to tell him how sorry I was to have been so rude."

She was silent for a moment before she said:

"He remarked how fortunate you were to have been left what I understand is a large fortune, a lovely house, and some very fine horses."

Daniela felt this was rather embarrassing, but her stepmother went on:

"Of course, like me, you are on an allowance until you are married, but I am sure it will not be very long before some charming, handsome young man steals your heart."

"I . . . I am in no . . . hurry," Daniela said quickly.

She was about to say that she hoped one day to find somebody she could love in the same way that her mother had loved her father.

Then she realised it would be tactless and merely added:

"I shall be . . . living very quietly . . . of course . . . while I am in . . . mourning."

37

It was then she remembered she had only one black gown.

"I suppose," she said tentatively, "there would be no time to . . . buy any more . . . black before we . . . leave tomorrow? I have only this one gown which the Mother Superior . . . bought for me and the coat that goes with it."

"It will be enough," her stepmother said, "and I am sure you will find plenty of beautiful gowns in Bond Street."

"Yes, of course," Daniela agreed, thinking if she was at home she would see no one.

Doubtless she could wear one of her white gowns with a black sash until she had time to go shopping.

"The Solicitors told me," her stepmother was saying, "that they will be coming tomorrow at half-past-eight to collect the coffin, and there will be a carriage for us to follow behind it to the Station. I am sure, dear child, as you have a long journey before you, you would be wise to have dinner in bed."

"In bed?" Daniela repeated in surprise.

"I am so sorry to leave you again," her stepmother went on, "but I have remembered that I am to have dinner with some old friends, and I do not like to disappoint them."

"No, of course not," Daniela agreed.

At the same time, she felt it rather strange.

She, however, went up to her bedroom, and a maid who was French came to help her undress.

"Will you please call me tomorrow morning at seven o'clock?" Daniela asked.

She thought she would get dressed quickly and pray once again beside her father's coffin before they put it on the hearse.

The French maid promised she would not be late, and then a footman brought Daniela dinner upstairs on a tray which the maid brought into the bedroom.

Daniela did not eat it in bed, as she thought it uncomfortable.

She sat, instead, on the side of the *chaise longue* and had the tray put on a small table beside her.

She had found it difficult to eat the plain food at the Convent when she was so unhappy after learning of her father's death.

The dinner she was offered tonight, however, was very different.

She knew her father had employed a good Chef, and she wondered if her stepmother would continue to live in this house.

Perhaps, she thought, it would be too expensive.

However, she did not wish to think of the woman who had taken her mother's place, and thought instead about going home to England.

How exciting it would be to see the horses she had always loved and the dogs that had followed her father everywhere he went.

When she had finished her dinner there was really nothing else she could do but get into bed.

It would be sensible, she thought, to try to sleep well knowing there was a long journey ahead of her.

Moreover, when they arrived there would be the emotional upset of talking to so many relatives and friends, who had loved her father and would be distressed at his death.

'I must be brave so that he is proud of me,' Daniela thought.

The maid who had taken away her tray came back.

"Before Her Ladyship left, *M'mselle*," she said, "she asked me to make you a *tisane* which will help you to sleep."

"It is very kind of her to think of it," Daniela said, "but I want nothing."

"I know Her Ladyship would be very disappointed," the maid said, "and this is a very nice *tisane*. In fact, Her Ladyship mixed it herself, and I only had to add a little warm water to it."

As she started to pour out the *tisane* into a glass she looked at Daniela and said pleadingly:

"Please drink it, *M'mselle*, otherwise *Madame* will be angry with me for not looking after you properly."

Because it seemed churlish to refuse, Daniela drank the *tisane* and quickly fell asleep.

She paused as she came to this part of the narrative, and the Marquis, who had been listening with an unflagging interest, asked:

"What happened then?"

"When I woke, I found it was quite late in the next day," Daniela replied, "and I was very ill."

The Marquis stared at her.

"Ill?" he questioned. "Do you mean the woman drugged you as she must have drugged your father?"

"She not only drugged me," Daniela said, "but I was so ill that there was no question of my going to England."

"But she had gone with your father's coffin?"

"Yes, she left with the Solicitors, and for two days I was unable to think clearly. I felt so desperately ill that I insisted on seeing a Doctor."

"And what did he say?" the Marquis enquired.

"He could not diagnose exactly what was wrong with me, but he gave me some medicine which merely made me sleepy, so after two doses I did not take any more."

"How long was your stepmother away?"

"She returned five days later, and by that time I was just

well enough to get out of bed and lie on the *chaise longue*."

"I can hardly believe it!" the Marquis exclaimed.

"I could not believe it myself," Daniela said, "until she told me that she would not allow me to go back to England."

"How could she stop you?" the Marquis asked.

"Very easily," Daniela replied, "as I was never allowed to be . . . alone."

She saw the Marquis was looking incredulous, and explained:

"Her Lady's-maid, a strange, unpleasant woman who looked like a witch and had been with her for many years, was my jailor!"

She drew in her breath before she continued:

"Maria sat with me when I was alone, escorted me if I went for a walk, and never left me unless my stepmother was with me."

"It seems incredible!" the Marquis murmured.

"That is what I thought when I was well enough to think clearly," Daniela said.

"But your relatives—surely they enquired about you?"

"If they did, I was not told about it, and when I wrote to them I soon realised my letters were not posted."

"Did you not try to see the Solicitor?" the Marquis enquired.

"I thought of it, but soon after she returned, my stepmother made it quite clear what she expected of me."

"And what was that?"

"I was to keep her by spending what money I had, and, of course, I could obtain what I asked for from the Trustees."

Daniela was silent for a moment before she continued:

"She dictated a letter I wrote to Mr. Meadowfield and I found it difficult to think of any way I could escape from her . . . until I saw you! That was when I came here. But when we . . . arrived something . . . terrible happened!''

"Tell me about it," the Marquis said.

"I am sure you find it . . . very hard to . . . believe what I am . . . saying," Daniela answered, "but I swear to you on . . . everything I hold . . . sacred that . . . every word I have . . . told you is . . . the truth.''

"I believe you," the Marquis said, "but I have to hear the end of this extraordinary story.''

"We stayed in Paris for a few weeks," Daniela replied, "and for two of them I was not really well enough to do anything but what my stepmother told me to do. Then one day, when I came downstairs feeling better, though at the same time frightened, she said:

" 'I think we should leave Paris. There are too many people nosing about and showing interest in what is happening to you.'

"I felt a sudden hope that perhaps the people in England were asking about me.

" 'What I have decided we will do,' my stepmother went on, 'is to go to Baden-Baden.'

"I stared at her in astonishment and she said:

" 'It is very amusing at this time of the year. I am sure you will find some young people who will interest you, and of course there will be the Casino, the races, and the Théâtre, these are things which I cannot take you to here.'

"I wondered if that was because I was in mourning or because she did not want me to be seen.

"Then she went on:

" 'Baden-Baden is a different world, where visitors come from all over Europe. You and I will enjoy ourselves without being encumbered by the ghosts of the past.'

"I knew she was thinking of Papa, but I did not wish to

42

be rude to her when she was being so unexpectedly pleasant, so I said nothing.

" 'What we will do,' she went on, 'is forget everything we have endured, and that includes being in mourning.'

"I looked at her in surprise, and she said:

" 'When the sun is shining, who wants to look like a drab crow? We will wear pretty gowns that will make men pay you compliments and bring a smile to your lips.'

"What she was saying was so surprising that I could only stare at her, and she said:

" 'We are going to what for us will be a new world, with new people, so you must forget for the moment that your name is Brooke, and I shall no longer be your father's wife.'

" 'What are you saying?' I exclaimed. 'It does not make sense to me!

" 'It does to me,' my stepmother replied. 'I intend to be the *Comtesse* de Bellevue, a name which I have always thought sounds very romantic.'

"I just looked at her, and she said:

" 'Because you look so English, you had better be English and the daughter of my first husband, who, unfortunately, died many years before I re-married. You can choose yourself any English name you like so long as it is not Brooke!'

"I found it hard to understand what she was saying, but when I did I said:

" 'Of course not! How could I be anything other than Papa's daughter? And anyway, I do not want to go to Baden-Baden! As I have already told you, I want to go home.'

" 'And I have no intention of letting you do so!' my stepmother said.

"It was the first time she had spoken so positively, but I had been so certain that she was determined to prevent me from returning to England that I had not raised the matter before.''

Daniela shut her eyes. She could see her stepmother's face all too clearly.

She knew by the way she half-closed her eyes that she was thinking of something unpleasant . . . something that would frighten her.

Because she was ashamed of herself for being afraid she said:

"Now I am feeling better, Stepmama, I wish to go to England, to my home and to my relations, and I intend to leave tomorrow!''

Lady Seabrooke threw back her head and laughed.

"Do you really think that possible?'' she asked.

"Of course it is!'' Daniela insisted. ''Perhaps you will allow one of the house-maids to travel with me, and I will, of course, send her back as soon as I reach my home, and will pay her for her services.''

"I have no doubt you would do that,'' Lady Seabrooke said sarcastically, ''but it just happens to be something I will not allow you to do!''

"I do not think you will be able to stop me,'' Daniela said. ''After all, I am eighteen, and I have relations who will look after me as Papa would wish them to do.''

"But I have already told you that you cannot see them, and you cannot go to England,'' Lady Seabrooke said.

She spoke so positively that Daniela just stared at her, wondering how she could reply.

"I thought you were intelligent,'' Lady Seabrooke said scathingly. ''Surely you understand that as your father is dead, I am now your Guardian, and you must do as I say?''

It was something that had never entered Daniela's mind, and for the moment she was speechless.

Then as she knew her stepmother was looking at her mockingly, she said:

"I do not think that legally is true!"

"On the contrary," Lady Seabrooke replied, "I have taken legal advice, and I assure you that as your father is dead, I am your natural Guardian by both French and English Law. You can only get rid of me, my dear little Stepdaughter, when you marry."

There was something in the way she said the last words that made Daniela more frightened than she was already.

It was as if her instinct told her that her stepmother was already plotting her marriage, and that was why they were going to Baden-Baden.

"I was frightened . . . very frightened," she said to the Marquis, "but there was nothing I could do but obey her and come here."

"Was there nobody you could appeal to in Paris?" the Marquis asked. "What about the French Solicitor?"

"I thought of him, of course, and also the Mother Superior," Daniela replied. "But I was locked in my room at night and never allowed out of the house."

The Marquis gave an exclamation beneath his breath, but he did not interrupt, and Daniela went on:

"A Dressmaker came to the house and my stepmother ordered an enormous amount of clothes which I knew I would have to pay for. I refused firmly to have anything that was coloured, and she compromised by letting me wear white, but I was not allowed a black sash or anything that suggested I was in mourning."

" 'White is quite correct for a young girl,' she said airily.

"She herself chose all the colours of the rainbow, and gowns that seemed to me astronomically expensive."

Daniela looked at the Marquis pleadingly.

"I know it must seem ridiculous to you that I could not get anyone to help me. I did think of appealing to the Dressmaker, but they all seemed to know my stepmother, and I thought she would merely say that I was hysterical, or perhaps given to delusions! The only thing I could do was just to agree to what she wished."

"So you came here," the Marquis said.

"We arrived, and by that time, because it was hopeless to argue against anything she suggested, I called myself by my mother's maiden name, which was Lyndon."

The Marquis frowned.

"I have met your aunt, Lady Compton, and I am sure she would be horrified to know of the position you are now in."

"I am sure she would be if there was any way I could communicate with her," Daniela said.

The Marquis did not speak and she went on:

"My stepmother told me before we arrived here that there were few English people in Baden-Baden, and if she found me speaking to any of them, she would take me away and have me locked up in a Lunatic Asylum!"

"I cannot believe that!" the Marquis said sharply.

"It is true!" Daniela said. "But then she has had a . . . better . . . idea . . . and one which will benefit herself . . . enormously."

"And what is that?"

"That I should be . . . married! My money will then be in the hands of my . . . husband whom she will . . . choose and . . . control!"

chapter three

THE horror in Daniela's voice was very evident, and after a moment the Marquis said quietly:

"At least that is something you can refuse to do."

"How can . . . I be . . . certain?" she asked. "After all, Papa was . . . married and had . . . no idea it had . . . happened until he . . . woke up next morning to find . . . she was . . . his wife!"

That was something the Marquis had momentarily forgotten.

He realised that if Esmé Blanc, and it was difficult to think of her by any other name, had pulled the trick off once, she might certainly try to do so again.

Because it all seemed so incredible, after several seconds of silence he asked:

"Can you be absolutely sure that this is her intention?"

"I thought when we . . . first came to . . . Baden-Baden

that is what my stepmother . . . intended,'' Daniela replied,
"and like you I thought it would be easy to say . . . no
to . . . any man who . . . proposed to me. Then last night
I . . . overheard . . . something which has made me . . .
even more afraid.

"What was that?" the Marquis enquired.

Daniela explained to him that they were staying in an
expensive Suite at the Stephanie Hotel.

As she would be paying, her stepmother had insisted on
the very best that was available, and they were on the First
Floor.

She had taken for herself the largest and most luxurious
of the bedrooms. Next to it was a Sitting-Room, beyond
which there was a smaller but quite comfortable room for
Daniela.

On the other side of her own room Lady Seabrooke had
installed her Lady's-Maid, Maria.

As it was impossible for Maria to accompany Daniela in
the evening when they went to the Casino, her stepmother
instructed her to keep close beside her.

If she disobeyed she would be punished in a manner which
would be very painful.

Daniela was aware that she was threatening to beat her.

Every nerve in her body shrank not only from the pain,
but also the humiliation.

She had therefore obediently stood behind her stepmother's chair.

Lady Seabrooke gambled in high stakes, losing a large
amount of the money which Daniela knew she would have
to finance eventually.

Before sitting down at the gambling table, Lady Seabrooke had scrutinised everybody in the Casino.

She had found a number of acquaintances.

Daniela had been aware that the women were fantastically gowned in the same way as her stepmother, their faces rouged and powdered.

A great number of them, she thought, spoke in a manner which told her they were not ladies.

She suspected they belonged to the *Demi-Monde*.

She was, however, too nervous to say so and was aware that what her stepmother was really looking for was a man.

There were, Daniela saw, a number of very distinguished gentlemen in the Casino.

Some of them were escorting the over-dressed and over-painted Courtesans whom her stepmother had greeted.

But though Daniela heard one or two of the women refer to her as "Madame Blanc," the gentlemen to whom she was introduced had either turned to talk to somebody else, or gone to the tables to gamble.

Last night they dined alone in the attractive Dining-Room of the Stephanie.

Afterwards they had gone to the Casino. Her stepmother had obviously found the man she had been seeking.

As they entered the Salle Louis-Quatorze, she gave a cry of delight and appeared to fling herself at a man standing just inside the door.

He was watching newcomers in a scrutinising way which did not seem quite natural.

He was slim, dark, and so obviously French that Daniela was not surprised when her stepmother said:

"Let me introduce you, Daniela, to an old friend and a very charming man, the *Comte* André de Sauzan."

She spoke the words slowly and distinctly.

Then she looked at the Frenchman out of the corners of her eyes as if she were sharing a joke with him.

"*Enchanté, Mademoiselle!*" the *Comte* said, and bowed.

Lady Seabrooke linked her arm through his, saying in a low voice that Daniela could only just hear:

"I have so much to tell you, and it will be, I assure you, very much to your advantage."

There was such a crowd and so much noise going on in the Casino that Daniela did not hear any more.

But the *Comte* stayed beside them all the evening and they returned to the Stephanie rather earlier than usual.

Daniela was relieved, as she had no wish to gamble and she found it irritating to watch her stepmother gambling with her money in an extravagant manner.

She knew that when Esmé Seabrooke lost, she would not worry, knowing who would have to pay.

They went straight up to the Suite and Daniela was sent to bed.

Maria was waiting for her.

As usual, she was disagreeable, making it clear that it was a nuisance to have to maid two ladies and, where Daniela was concerned, act as jailor.

Having locked her in without saying goodnight, Maria went to her own room.

Daniela gave a sigh of relief.

As if it were not insulting enough to be locked in, her stepmother had decreed that all her clothes were to be kept in Maria's room just in case she had any idea of trying to escape.

It would be impossible, she knew, for her to walk about the Hotel wearing only a diaphanous nightgown which had been bought for her in Paris.

It was equally impossible to climb out of the window even if she had been prepared to risk her neck in doing so.

She was not tired, and as she did not want to sleep she pulled back the curtains and looked out at the night.

The Hotel had in front of it a garden which sloped down to the banks of the Oos, over which there were picturesquely designed bushes.

From her window Daniela could see the moonlight turning the water to silver and glittering through the leaves in the trees.

Above them there was the sky filled with stars.

It was so lovely that she had a longing to be outside instead of caged behind walls which to all intents and purposes were the bars of a prison.

Then she remembered that in the Sitting-Room of their Suite there was a French window which opened onto a balcony.

She wondered if she could go out there into the night air without anyone being aware of it.

The door of her bedroom communicated with the Sitting-Room.

Her stepmother's room was on the other side of it.

She knew that even if the door into the passage was unlocked, she would hardly run away in her nightgown.

Now, because she wanted just for a moment to feel free, she opened the communicating door very quietly.

She was sure that by this time the *Comte* had left, for otherwise she would have heard their voices, even if she could not distinguish what they were saying.

She was right.

He must have gone, for the Sitting-Room was in darkness.

The curtains covering the French windows had been pulled back, and one of the casements was opened onto the balcony.

Walking on tip-toe, just in case her stepmother should hear her, she crossed the room, making no sound on the soft carpet, and reached the window.

As she did so she heard a man's voice and stood still.

It was then she realised that the *Comte* was in her stepmother's bedroom.

It was a shock because when she had been introduced to him as an "old friend," it had never struck Daniela, in her innocence, that he was in fact Esmé Seabrooke's lover.

She had been shocked, horrified, and appalled that *Madame* Blanc had married her father in such a deceitful manner.

At the same time, he said she had pleaded with him, so she had supposed she in a way loved him.

Daniela had never come in contact with women who sold themselves to men simply for what they could get out of it in hard cash.

She found it hard, therefore, even though she disliked and despised her stepmother, to realise that in such a short time after her father's death she was in bed with another man.

For the moment she was stunned into immobility and could only stand listening to the *Comte*'s voice.

She could not hear what he said, but when her stepmother answered him there was no doubt that her voice was passionate.

It was very different from the hard, shrill tone in which she usually spoke to her.

Feeling disgusted and almost physically sick, Daniela pushed the window farther open and stepped out into the darkness.

She walked to where she was farthest from her stepmother's bedroom and could no longer hear their voices.

She found that her heart was beating agitatedly and her hands were cold, and she knew she was suffering from shock.

Then she told herself it was foolish when she was trying to escape to worry about what her stepmother was doing.

"I must get . . . back to . . . England—I must!" she said, looking up at the stars. "Help me, Papa, help me. You cannot . . . leave me . . . here with this . . . terrible woman!"

Daniela went on praying both to her father and her mother, feeling that wherever they were they would hear her, and somehow show her a way of escape.

She suddenly became aware that the wind had risen, which was moving the leaves of the trees, and since she was wearing nothing but a nightgown, she felt cold.

She told herself she must go to bed and reluctantly moved back along the balcony to the window.

Careful to make no noise, she stepped through it onto the carpet.

As she did so she saw there was a long streak of light coming from the corner of the room where the communicating door led into her stepmother's bedroom.

She realised that the wind blowing through the window must have opened the door, but the occupants were unaware of it.

They were talking, and now Daniela could hear what they said quite clearly.

"You must agree that my plan is brilliant!" she heard her stepmother say, her voice no longer low and passionate.

"I am afraid that somebody might be aware that Yvonne is still alive," the *Comte* replied.

"You have not seen her for years, and you know as well as I do that you have changed your name."

The *Comte* laughed.

"As you have changed yours!"

"It is something we can always do again," her stepmother said with a giggle.

"Nevertheless, I have no wish to get into trouble."

"If you do, you will have enough money to buy your way out of it.

"It would be wise to go to England and take over the house and estate. I had a good look at it when I was there, and I can assure you it is magnificent and very much in the grand manner!"

There was silence, then Esmé added:

"I shall be with you, and we shall be very happy, as we have always been."

"Are you quite certain, Esmé, it is the only way we can obtain her money?" the *Comte* enquired.

"The only way, unless we wait until she is twenty-five."

He laughed.

"And we cannot wait," he said. "There is no need for me to tell you that as usual I am down to my last franc! I was looking for a chicken to pluck when you came in to-night."

"This is not a chicken, but a pot of gold!" Esmé replied. "We can share it together and be comfortable for the rest of our lives!"

Again there was a pause before the *Comte* said:

"All right. I have little alternative but to agree, but I am not being married as a Catholic. I have no wish, if there is any fuss, to be excommunicated!"

"No, of course not," Esmé replied soothingly. "I will arrange everything at the Protestant Church, where to you it will not be a real marriage."

"You are very clever, *ma chère*."

"That is what I want you to think, as you always have! Oh, André, kiss me! I cannot tell you how wonderful it is to be with you again."

The whole horror of what they were doing awoke Daniela

from the stupor which had held her spellbound as she listened to their conversation.

As she realised that to be discovered would be disastrous, she moved slowly on tip-toe across the room to the door which led her into her bedroom.

Only when she had shut it slowly and carefully did she run to what seemed the security of her own bed and pull the sheets up to her chin.

Could it really be true, what she had heard?

Could her stepmother really be intending to marry her to a man who was already married so that they could live in the house that had always been her home and spend her father's money?

It was almost impossible for her to believe that any woman could sink so low and behave so abominably.

'I will denounce her! I will tell the world what she is like!' Daniela thought.

Then she knew with a feeling of horror that it was unlikely anyone would believe her even if she could find somebody to talk to.

She knew also that as her stepmother had done to her father, she would be quite capable of drugging her.

Then she would have her married without being aware of what was happening to her.

As she lay in bed, going over and over what she had heard, she asked herself if, because they had been speaking in French, she might have misunderstood their intentions.

Then she knew that she was not mistaken.

Unless she could find some way to prevent it, she would be taken to the Protestant Church and married to a man who would be a Bigamist.

She was also afraid that if she tried to denounce her stepmother and the *Comte*, she might be murdered if they thought anyone would believe her accusations against them.

"What . . . can I . . . do? Oh, God, what can . . . I do?"

Only as the hours passed did she know that only her prayers could help her, and that by some miracle she would be rescued.

All through the next day Daniela became more and more aware of the danger she was in.

Her stepmother did not rise until nearly luncheontime.

It was twelve noon when the *Comte* arrived and came up to the Suite.

Champagne was waiting for him, besides a pot of *pâté de foie gras* and another of caviar.

Now, as Daniela looked at him more closely in the daylight, she thought that her father would never have trusted him, nor would her mother.

There was something about him which made her shudder.

When she touched his hand, the vibrations from it told her he was an evil man.

He was not as young as he had seemed last night.

She thought he must be getting on for forty.

Because he was slim and there were no grey hairs on his dark head, he looked younger.

It was, she thought, his eyes that betrayed him.

When he paid her compliments she knew by the expression in his eyes that he was merely thinking of her fortune, and how pleasant it would be to spend it.

"I thought today we would go to the races," her stepmother was saying.

"That is what I knew you would want to do," the *Comte* answered, "and I am sure *Mademoiselle* will enjoy seeing some of the finest horses in Europe."

"You sound too formal," her stepmother said archly.

"Do call her Daniela. I want you two people whom I love to become friends."

"Of course I shall be honoured," the *Comte* said, "and Daniela is a very pretty name."

To Daniela it was an agony to listen to this man talking to her as if he were genuinely interested in her as a woman!

All he wanted was to share with her stepmother the money they were intent on stealing from her.

Later they had gone to the races.

But Daniela was not entranced, as she would have been ordinarily, by the horses that were, as the *Comte* had said, some of the finest in Europe.

The on-lookers were in their own way almost as magnificent.

The Owners, who had come from Paris and every adjacent country, were most of them aristocrats.

The Ladies, in gowns that were a tribute to the French Couturiers, might each of them have played the lead in the New Théâtre.

Despite being desperately worried and afraid, Daniela could not help looking round at what seemed to her more like a pageant than reality.

It was then she had seen coming from the stands to look at the horses parading before the next race a woman who was even more spectacularly dressed than the others.

She was not exactly beautiful, but as she walked past, Daniela could see she had a fascinating face.

She was somehow different from the other women who were looking at her with undisguised jealousy.

Then Daniela heard her say:

"I'll bet you ten thousand pounds that you can't beat the *Duc*'s horse!"

Daniela realised with surprise that she was speaking in

English and that her voice, while young and gay, was also somewhat common.

Then she heard the man who was with her reply:

"Done! And if you lose, Cora, I shall expect you to pay up."

It was his deep voice which made Daniela look at him, and she realised that he was in fact extremely handsome.

She was, however, not concerned with his looks but his having spoken in the same way that her father might have done.

There was something about him, perhaps because of his nationality, that made her feel her father was near her and helping her.

'Perhaps if I could speak to him, he would tell me what to do,' she thought.

Then as he walked away beside the woman whom he had called Cora, she knew despairingly that she would be unable to approach him.

When later the Gentleman's horse won the big race by a head, she learned who he was, and was also told somewhat harshly by her stepmother of his involvement with Cora Pearl.

"How that woman can be so successful I do not know!" she said in an envious voice. "If you ask me, she uses Black Magic to get the men into her clutches!"

"There is no doubt they are mesmerised by her," the *Comte* said. "Have you heard of her latest gamble?"

"If she has won any more money, then I do not want to hear about it," Esmé snapped, "but I expect you will not tell me anyway!"

The *Comte* laughed.

"We all know Cora Pearl spends a fortune on entertaining, and has one of the best Chefs in Paris."

He stopped speaking a moment before continuing:

"The other day she wagered her guests she would give them some meat that none of them would dare to carve."

He paused, and Esmé said:

"I cannot imagine what that could be."

"It was quite simple," the *Comte* replied. "She had herself served on a huge silver salver carried by four men. She was naked except for a sprinkling of parsley!"

Esmé did not laugh. Instead, she said sourly:

"Why did I not think of that?"

Daniela turned away.

How could her father's wife wish to do anything, so immodest, so unpleasant?

When they returned to the Stephanie, she found herself thinking of the Marquis of Crowle.

Vaguely at the back of her mind she could remember hearing his name when she was in England.

That night they had dinner at the Casino and she thought that, if the Marquis were there, perhaps she would get a chance to speak to him.

She could then beg him to help her because she was her father's daughter.

She knew that her stepmother would be furious if she called herself anything but Daniela Lyndon, which was the name under which she was registered at the Hotel.

But perhaps the Marquis would remember her father and feel because they were both English that he should help her.

Her stepmother seated herself at a Roulette Table and said to the *Comte*:

"I will play first, and you look after Daniela. Then we will change places."

"It will be a pleasure!" the *Comte* said with a smile.

He was standing behind Esmé's chair, watching her place her stakes.

First she lost, then she won, and obviously did not wish to give up her place now that she had a small pile of chips in front of her.

It was then Daniela saw the Marquis rise from another table in the room.

She watched him change what must have been a large amount of chips for paper money.

As he walked out of the Casino, she realised he was going into the garden.

She turned to the *Comte*.

"I wonder if I might have something to drink?" she asked. "It is very hot in here."

"You are quite right," he said, "and I expect Esmé would like something too."

He bent forward to say to her:

"Would you like a glass of champagne?"

"I would love it!" she replied.

The *Comte* looked around for one of the servants in knee-breeches and smart uniform.

He saw one at the far end of the room, and as he walked towards him Daniela knew this was her opportunity.

Quickly, like a small animal escaping from the hunt, she pushed through the crowd of on-lookers standing around the Roulette Tables.

She found her way to the French windows which opened onto the garden.

"They will be . . . looking for me," she said now to the Marquis, "and they will be very . . . angry if I am . . . found here with . . . you."

For a moment he did not speak, and she said in a piteous little voice:

"You . . . do understand . . . I am . . . frightened?"

"Of course I do," he replied, and "and I must help you to escape."

"Will you really do that?"

Daniela clasped her hands together and there was a light in her eyes that seemed to rival the stars.

"It is not going to be easy," the Marquis said cautiously, "but I cannot allow your father's daughter and an English-woman to be treated in such a disgraceful fashion!"

"That is what I . . . hoped and . . . prayed you would say," Daniela answered.

"But you do understand," he said, "that if I accuse your stepmother or de Sauzan of a crime they have not yet committed, they will deny it, and it will only be your word against theirs."

"B-but . . . I cannot marry him! Supposing his wife is . . . not alive after all . . . and it is . . . l-legal?"

"I find it hard to believe that de Sauzan, however criminally-minded he may be, would actually become a Bigamist!" the Marquis said.

"Nevertheless, I am sure that is what they are planning . . . and if we are . . . married in a Protestant Church, perhaps, as he is a Catholic, for him it will not be a marriage."

She hesitated over the words. Then she said in a voice the Marquis could hardly hear:

"I . . . I could not let him . . . touch me!"

"No, of course not, and that is why we have to act quickly. For the moment, I am not certain what I can do."

He remembered as he spoke that he had intended to leave Baden-Baden the day after tomorrow, but now he might have to stay longer.

One thing was quite certain, and that was that he must take Daniela with him.

He had no idea how he could do so.

If, as she had said, Esmé Seabrooke had taken legal advice and she was genuinely Daniela's Guardian, the Law both in England and, he supposed, in France, gave the Guardian of a minor the same power as that of a father or mother.

This meant that a Guardian could do very much as he or she liked.

When it came to marriage, there was no doubt it could take place without the consent of the bride, who would have no say in the choice of her husband.

As the Marquis was thinking, he was aware that Daniela was looking at him, her eyes very revealing in the light from the sky.

She was also, the Marquis was aware, very attractive.

He was not interested in young girls, and never had been.

But if he had to play the Knight Gallant to a woman, it made it seem more credible that she should be young and lovely rather than otherwise.

"I feel," Daniela was saying in her soft, musical voice, "as if Papa has sent you to me . . . at a moment when I was so desperate . . . and had begun to think the . . . only way I could . . . escape such a horror would be to . . . d-drown myself!"

"You are not to talk like that!" the Marquis admonished her. "I am sure your father, if nothing else, would want you to be brave, and certainly to do nothing so wicked as to commit suicide."

"I expected you would think like that, as Papa would have," Daniela said, "but . . . it is not only that the *Comte* is a . . . horrid . . . evil man. He also . . . belongs to . . . my stepmother.''

The Marquis thought it was what he might have expected, although it had not in fact entered his mind.

He was aware that, because she was so young and had been brought up in a Convent, she was deeply shocked at the idea of her stepmother taking a lover.

She had been shocked in the same way when she found out that Esmé was staying with her father.

He knew it was a long time since he had met anyone so innocent and unspoilt.

It also flashed through his mind that it would be a disaster for Daniela to meet anybody like Cora Pearl.

Or to realise the depths of depravity to which the *Grandes Courtesans* of Paris could sink.

Aloud he said:

''What we have to do, Daniela, is to be very clever about this. Whatever happens, your stepmother must not be aware that I am trying to help you.''

He paused before he went on:

''But if events are speeded up, or if anything happens unexpectedly and you wish to tell me about it, try to get a message to the Villa d'Horizon.''

''Is that where you are staying?'' Daniela asked.

''It is,'' the Marquis replied. ''When I decided to bring my horses to Baden-Baden, a friend lent me his Villa, as he has gone to Monte Carlo.''

''The Villa d'Horizon,'' Daniela repeated to herself.

She was thinking as she did so that it would be very difficult to find a way of communicating with the Marquis.

At the same time, it was somehow comforting to know where he would be.

''I think perhaps—'' the Marquis began.

As he spoke there was the sound of voices.

"She must be here somewhere!" a woman exclaimed.

The Marquis was aware that Daniela had stiffened and said quickly:

"If that is your stepmother, say you have been sitting here alone because you felt faint."

Then with the swiftness of an athlete the Marquis rose from the seat and disappeared into the bushes behind him.

One moment he was there—the next he had gone.

Daniela sat still without moving except that she turned her face up to the stars.

Esmé Seabrooke, accompanied by the *Comte*, came in sight, moving quickly over the green lawn, looking to right and left.

When she saw Daniela she gave an exclamation:

"There she is!"

She walked quickly across the intervening space, and when she reached Daniela she said disagreeably:

"Where have you been? What do you mean by coming here by yourself and giving us all a fright?"

"I . . . I am sorry, Stepmama," Daniela replied, "but . . . I suddenly felt faint . . . and came into the garden to get some air."

"I told you she could come to no harm," the *Comte* said testily.

"All the same, she might have," Esmé Seabrooke answered. "I warned you not to leave her!"

"Well, here she is, safe and sound!" the *Comte* replied. "I suggest, Daniela, you come back to the Casino and have a glass of champagne."

"Yes . . . thank you," Daniela said, "if that is what you wish me to do."

"In future you will do as you are told," Esmé Seabrooke

said angrily. "You have given me a shock, and I had to leave the tables just when I was winning!"

"I . . . I am . . . sorry."

"And so you should be!"

Esmé Seabrooke paused for a moment.

Then, as if she thought she should say something different, she added:

"You upset André by running off like that—didn't she?"

"Yes, indeed, I was extremely perturbed," the *Comte* agreed. "Anyone as lovely as you might easily have got into trouble being alone in the garden with so many strange men about."

Daniela did not answer, and as if he felt he must draw attention to himself, the *Comte* went on:

"If I had found that you had run away with some handsome stranger, I should have been jealous—very jealous!"

"What . . . I would like to do," Daniela said as if she had not heard him, "is to go to bed. I have a headache because it has been so hot."

"Really! How can you be so selfish?" Esmé asked angrily. "You know André and I want to play at the tables, and most girls would find the excitement of the Casino enjoyable."

She would have said more, but the *Comte* intervened.

"If Daniela has a headache, we should take her home," he said.

He paused before continuing:

"If you want to return, I will bring you back and, quite frankly, I feel it rather frustrating to be in the Casino and not be in a position to play."

He gave Esmé a very revealing glance as he spoke.

Daniela thought it was unlikely her stepmother would

give him any money until he had done what she wanted him to do.

As this was something she did not wish to think about, she moved a little quicker so that she walked ahead of them.

As they whispered to each other behind her, she did not even bother to listen.

All she could feel was that her heart was leaping with joy because the Marquis had said he would help her.

Somehow, however difficult it might be, she was sure he would find a way of doing so.

As they walked through the Casino she did not see the crowds around the Roulette and Baccarat Tables.

Nor did she notice the beauty of the rooms and the dazzling light from the chandeliers.

She was saying in her heart over and over again:

"Thank You, God, thank You for letting . . . me find . . . him."

chapter four

THE Marquis waited some appreciable time before Daniela, escorted by her stepmother and the *Comte*, disappeared towards the Casino.

He was thinking again that he had never in his life heard such an extraordinary story.

And yet, because he was very perceptive, he was convinced that Daniela was telling him the truth.

It was, he thought, a warning to all men, even himself, not to become involved too deeply with the Courtesans of Paris.

Like Esmé Blanc, they would sink to any depths to get their own way.

He could understand that for her the idea of becoming the wife of an English nobleman had been irresistible.

At the same time, it seemed incredible that having

achieved her objective, she should have allowed Lord Sea-brooke to become involved in a duel.

It might have been accidental, but from what Daniela told him about it, he had a feeling that Esmé had deliberately contrived to put her rich husband in a dangerous position.

All this led to the question as to what he should do about Daniela.

He had no wish whatsoever to be involved in a scandal.

He was certain that the new Lady Seabrooke would not hesitate to blackmail him in any way she could.

If it was to her advantage, she might even bring a Law Suit against him.

"What the Devil am I to do?" he asked himself as he walked slowly back to the Casino.

He could not help thinking that if he were sensible, he would leave Baden-Baden and its problems and return to England alone.

Then he knew that despite his cynicism he had been very touched by the terror he had heard in Daniela's voice.

He knew also that she was young, innocent of the world, and to all intents and purposes completely alone.

It struck him that he could contact her relations and tell them to send one of her male relatives over to Baden-Baden to sort things out.

Then he had the uncomfortable feeling that there would not be time for this.

If Daniela was already married, it would be very difficult to prove it was illegal.

He could also remember the horror in her voice as she had said:

"I . . . I could not let him . . . touch me!"

The Marquis almost prided himself on being ruthless and quite unconcerned with other people's feelings.

Yet he knew this was the cry of a child in the dark, and that he could not ignore it.

He walked into the Casino, hoping that Daniela would have left.

He saw with relief there was no sign of her or her step-mother, nor of the dubious *Comte*.

He could, however, see Cora Pearl sipping champagne and being entertained by three men.

He suspected that she had already lost the money he had given her and was waiting for more.

She was looking fantastic and alluring, in a gown which was immodestly low and ornamented with Birds of Paradise.

He guessed it had cost more than a year's salary of anyone employed in the Casino.

Her necklace was spectacular, as were her ear-rings, bracelets, and the crescent moon she was wearing in her hair.

As the Marquis joined the party, one of the men exclaimed:

"Hello, Crowle, we missed you and wondered where you had gone."

"It was hot," the Marquis said briefly, "and I went into the garden."

"I only hope she was not cool!" one of the other men said in French.

He laughed at his own flippant remark.

The Marquis was ordering himself some champagne and did not reply.

The conversation was amusing and witty, usually at the expense of somebody else.

An hour later the Marquis said to Cora:

"Let me take you home. I am tired, and there is another day's racing tomorrow."

She looked up at him with an obvious invitation in her eyes and was not certain when she rose to her feet whether he had answered or not.

When they had driven away from the Casino in a comfortable carriage drawn by two horses, the Marquis asked:

"What do you know about a woman called Esmé Blanc?"

Cora Pearl raised her pencilled eye-brows before she replied:

"A two-penny tart with ambitions to get out of the sewer!"

The Marquis laughed.

However successful she had been, Cora had never lost her common accent or her Leicester Square way of speaking.

"Why are you interested?" she enquired.

"I understand she married an Englishman whom I knew," the Marquis replied, picking his words carefully.

"She married him, then contrived to get him murdered!" Cora answered.

It was like her, the Marquis thought, to know what he suspected himself.

"I should have thought that was a mistake," he said, "seeing that she would have been of some importance as Lady Seabrooke."

"All Esmé Blanc, which of course isn't her real name, has ever wanted," Cora replied, "is money. She wants to live in the same style as I do, but has no idea how to set about it."

"That I can understand," the Marquis said mockingly. "You are unique, Cora, as you well know."

"It's hardly a compliment to be imitated by women like Esmé Blanc, who at the moment is calling herself the *Comtesse* de Bellevue, and if there was ever a *Comte* of that name, I'll eat my hat!"

The Marquis laughed at the very English idiom which sounded strange in a foreign country.

"Now tell me about this man she was with tonight," the Marquis said, "*Comte* André de Sauzan."

"A reptile!" Cora exclaimed. "A procurer, blackmailer, a man whom I would not allow to cross the threshold of any house I own! He is dirt and should be in the gutter, where he belongs!"

She spoke so violently that the Marquis asked:

"What has he done to you?"

"He tried to steal something belonging to me," Cora replied, "but I caught him in the act, and told my servants to throw him out of the window. It happened to be closed and he was in hospital for several weeks."

The Marquis laughed again.

It was so like Cora, and he could visualise all too vividly what had happened.

"He and Esmé Blanc had a girl with them tonight," Cora said, as if recalling what she had hardly noticed before.

"That is right," the Marquis said.

"You can bet they're selling her to the highest bidder, and don't let it be you!"

"I shall look to you to protect me," the Marquis said with a smile.

The horses had stopped outside the Villa Mimosa, which one of Cora Pearl's admirers had given her several years earlier.

She had redecorated it several times, but the Marquis could not help being amused by the present appearance of her bedroom.

It was certainly sensational.

Everything was white—the walls, the curtains, the carpet, and the flowers.

The exception was the bed, which was huge and stood on two steps covered in white fur.

It was of black jet carved into the shape of a fantastic boat with the figure of a naked man holding the tiller.

The sheets, the pillows, and the blankets on the bed were all black, the cover being of priceless black ermine.

The Marquis knew no-one else could have thought of such an astonishing and compelling background.

As Cora lay naked on the black bed, her exquisite figure had the translucence of a pearl.

The Marquis answered the question in her eyes.

*   *   *

The first fingers of the dawn were coming up on the horizon as the Marquis walked the short way to the Villa d'Horizon.

It was very differently furnished, comfortable but masculine, with sporting pictures which he would have liked to own himself.

Before he got into the comfortable bed that was waiting for him, he washed away the cloying, seductive perfume which lingered on his body from his contact with Cora.

As he did so he told himself again that it was time he went home to England.

*   *   *

Although she was very tired, Daniela found it hard to sleep.

She kept thinking of the Marquis, knowing that, while he had promised to help her, it was not going to be easy.

When they got back to the Stephanie, she had gone at once to her bedroom, thinking her stepmother would want to be alone with the *Comte*.

But she followed her to say again how furious she was at her slipping away from the gambling-rooms and going into the garden by herself.

"Will you get it into your stupid head that you have to obey me?" she stormed. "If you behave like this another time, I will lock you in your room and make you stay here alone until I return."

Daniela thought of saying she would not mind that and would rather be alone than with the *Comte*.

Then she thought it would cause a scene.

The wisest thing she could do was to be apologetic.

"I am sorry if I upset you, Stepmama," she said.

"Well, you can show your sorrow by writing me a cheque," Esmé replied. "I want some money, and although you may not be aware of it, we cannot live here without it."

"But I gave you one thousand pounds when we arrived," Daniela protested, "and I have already spent most of my year's allowance in this last month!"

"You know as well as I do," her stepmother snapped, "that your Solicitors who call themselves Trustees will give you anything you ask for."

She hesitated for a moment before continuing:

"They would hardly allow you to be sued by your creditors. Write me a cheque for a thousand pounds and I will cash it at the Bank tomorrow."

There was nothing Daniela could do but take out her cheque-book and do what her stepmother told her.

She thought despairingly that if this went on, her father's fortune would soon be thrown away on needless extravagances.

Then she remembered the Marquis and told herself that once she could get home she would somehow be able to prevent her stepmother from draining away every penny she possessed.

When she had signed the cheque she held it out to her stepmother, who looked at it to make sure there were no mistakes, then walked towards the door.

"Now go to bed," she said, "and you had better behave tomorrow, or you will be sorry. That means you obey me—do you understand? You obey me in everything I tell you to do."

"I . . . I understand," Daniela murmured.

At the same time, she was frightened.

When her stepmother left the room, Maria came in to help her undress and take away her gown.

She left her nothing but a very thin nightgown in which she was to sleep.

There was not even a wrap or a negligee in the empty wardrobe.

As Daniela got into bed, she wondered whether if she wrapped herself in a blanket, there would be any chance of escaping.

The outside door was locked when Maria left her and she had no wish to go into the Sitting-Room as she had done the last night.

She knew that as her stepmother left through the communicating door, the *Comte* was waiting.

He had not said goodnight to her downstairs.

She tried not to think of them making love.

All she wanted to think about was in what way she could reach the Marquis if she was suddenly ordered to go to the Church.

"Help me, Papa, help me . . . again," she prayed. "I am sure it was through . . . you that I was able . . . to talk to him tonight, but it may not be . . . so easy another . . . time."

74

Finally she fell asleep and was dreaming that she was a child again when Maria came into the room to pull back the curtains.

Daniela did not open her eyes and said drowsily to Maria:

"Surely . . . it is . . . very early?"

"It's ten o'clock," Maria answered, "and *Madame* says you're to be up and dressed in your best gown by noon, and I am to bring you a bath."

Daniela drew in her breath.

She knew this meant danger.

Because she was English she was always asking for a bath, and there was inevitably a great commotion about it.

Could it be possible, she asked herself, that she was to be married today?

Quite suddenly she was panic-stricken.

For a moment she could think of nothing but that she should run away through the door that was now unlocked.

She would run down the stairs and escape while she had the chance.

Then she knew that was impossible wearing nothing but her nightgown, and she listened to Maria chatting to the *femme de chambre* about her bath.

The maid had a great deal to say about it.

Finally two of them came into the room with a circular bath which they set down on the hearth-rug.

They put a bath-mat beside it, and a large Turkish towel was laid ready on one of the chairs.

When the maids left the room Daniela knew they were waiting for the men to bring up the hot water and cold water in large cans.

It was then she had an idea.

Jumping out of bed, she went to the writing-desk, where there was a blotter filled with writing-paper headed with the name of the Hotel and a supply of envelopes.

Quickly she scribbled one short line:

*I think I am being married at noon please—please—
save me!*
       Daniela

She had to write it quickly while Maria was outside the room.

She put what she had written into an envelope and addressed it to the Marquis of Crowle at the Villa d'Horizon.

Then she went to the dressing-table and opening her jewel-box, took out a small diamond and pearl brooch which had belonged to her mother.

Her stepmother had made certain that she had no money of her own, saying it was quite unnecessary.

Although it hurt her to part with anything that had been her mother's, she knew that at the moment any sacrifice was worth while.

She got back into bed holding the note and the brooch under the sheet and watched the maids bringing in the water for her bath.

It was quite a laborious task.

First one maid came in with a pan of hot water which she had been handed outside by one of the men-servants who had carried it up the stairs.

She poured it into the bath.

Then the other maid who was younger and rather more attractive came in with a can of cold water.

Maria was still talking to the men outside who were obviously asking her how many more cans would be required by the fastidious English *M'mselle*.

She was sure she was replying that the French habit of

76

washing completely in a basin was far more reasonable.

The door was ajar, and as they were very intent on their conversation, Daniela slipped out of bed.

She went up to the young maid who was pouring water rather slowly into the bath in case she made it too cold.

Speaking in a low voice that only she could hear, she said:

"If you would take this note to the gentleman to whom it is addressed, I will give you this diamond and pearl brooch. It is real and very valuable."

The maid's eyes looked down at it with astonishment and stopped pouring the water.

"Help me . . . please . . . help me!" Daniela said. "It is very important . . . and I know the gentleman, if you ask him, will also give you some money."

"Shall I take it tonight, *M'mselle*?" the maid enquired.

"No, no!" Daniela said quickly. "Now! At once!"

She was afraid that Maria might come back.

As she spoke she slipped the envelope and the brooch into the pocket of the apron the maid was wearing.

"Hurry! Please . . . hurry!" she begged. "It means . . . everything in the world to me!"

As she spoke, Maria came back into the room and Daniela bent forward to put her hand into the bath-water as if she were testing it.

"I think that is the right temperature now," she said in an ordinary voice.

"You can have some more water if you want it," Maria said, "but I don't think it's necessary."

"No, it is all right," Daniela agreed.

The young maid was watching her.

"If that's all right, *M'mselle*," she said, "I'll take the can away."

She walked to the door.

When she reached it she looked back and gave Daniela a glance, and she thought, although she was not completely confident, that the maid would do as she had asked.

She was convinced as Maria shut the door behind her that if she did not do so, then she was doomed.

She took as long as she could to have her bath and was only half-dressed when her stepmother came into the room.

"Are you not ready yet?" she asked disagreeably. "I want Maria to do your hair, and she should have finished with you by now."

"I am sorry, Stepmama," Daniela replied, "but I did not know there was any particular hurry."

"We have an appointment," Lady Seabrooke said.

"An appointment?" Daniela repeated. "Where, and with whom?"

"There is no time to answer a lot of questions! Get dressed and I will send Maria back later with the gown you are to wear."

Daniela did not reply, but as if she had sensed that she was perturbed, her stepmother said to Maria:

"Lock the outside door and come to my bedroom."

She went into the Sitting-Room as she spoke and Daniela heard the *Comte*'s voice.

She knew then that he must have spent the night with her stepmother, finding it cheaper than staying elsewhere in the Town.

In a way she could understand that because he was desperate he could not reject her stepmother's plan to make him rich by marrying the girl whose fortune would become his the moment she was his wife.

She thought how degrading it would be to return to England with a husband whom she knew her relatives would disapprove the minute they met him.

Her stepmother, she was quite certain, had shocked them already.

It was an agony to think of Esmé Blanc, who she realised now was exactly like the women in the Casino, living in the house that had been her father's and mother's home.

She knew that what her stepmother admired and wanted would be very different in every way.

Even her choice of flowers would be different from those with which her mother had surrounded herself, and which had always seemed a part of her beauty.

Lilies, roses, the violets and primroses of Spring, the daffodils which made a golden carpet under the trees in the Park had pleased her mother.

But Esmé liked only orchids because they were expensive.

She wore them on her gowns in the daytime or carried them in the evening.

Green or purple, they always seemed to Daniela to symbolise greed.

She looked at herself in the mirror and saw she was ready except for her gown which had not yet been brought to her.

Then as she was putting the finishing touches to her hair Maria came back into the room.

She was carrying a white gown which looked to Daniela more like a dress for the evening than for the daytime.

"What is that?" she asked, turning round from the dressing-table.

"What do you think it is?" Maria asked unpleasantly. "You're lucky *Madame* could find you a wedding-gown in Baden-Baden!"

"A wedding-gown?" Daniela exclaimed.

She had suspected that was what it was, but somehow it was still a shock to be told so in words.

"You are going to be married," Maria said, "and if you ask me, it's a mistake doing it in so much of a hurry!"

"I will not be married!" Daniela exclaimed. "I refuse!"

As she spoke, her stepmother, dressed in one of her more fantastic gowns and wearing a hat covered in feathers, came into the room.

"Now, we don't want a scene!" she said sharply. "And if you start screaming, I'll give you something to drink which will prevent you from saying anything more!"

"You mean you will drug me as you drugged Papa!" Daniela retorted.

She thought her stepmother might be surprised, but instead she merely laughed.

"That's right, and he knew nothing until he woke up the next morning."

She paused before continuing:

"So you can take your choice. You can walk up the aisle on your own two feet and marry André in a dignified manner, or we can drug you!"

"I do not believe any Clergyman would marry a bride who cannot speak up for herself," Daniela said defensively.

"You will speak all right," her stepmother replied grimly, "but you'll not remember a thing!"

She paused for a moment before she said in a jeering tone:

"Every woman wants to remember her wedding-day, and if you're sensible, you'll remember yours, unlike your father, who had not the slightest idea what had happened to him until he found himself in bed with me!"

The way she spoke was so incredible that Daniela could only shut her eyes.

She felt that her stepmother's jeering voice was not real but part of some scurrilous lampoon.

"Come on, what's it to be?" she asked. "I'm giving you a choice, but whichever way you choose, the end'll be the same."

That was the answer, Daniela thought, but there was just a chance, a slender one, that the Marquis would save her.

"I will be married quietly," she said.

"I thought you would," her stepmother replied. "Now, hurry up and get ready. No man likes to be kept waiting."

She flounced from the room as she finished speaking, and Maria lifted the wedding-gown and put it over Daniela's head.

Then she produced a lace veil which she had carried over her arm and a wreath of orange-blossom.

She arranged it on Daniela's hair, fixing it in place with large hair-pins.

As she did so, Daniela looked at herself in the mirror and thought it could not be true that she was to be married against her will to her stepmother's lover.

She could not imagine anything could be more humiliating.

Because she was frightened, she could only pray that the *femme de chambre* had done as she had asked of her and by this time the Marquis had received her message.

* * *

In the Villa d'Horizon the Marquis had risen later than usual because it was six o'clock in the morning before he was finally in bed.

Before he fell asleep he thought of Daniela and decided he would make more enquiries that day about the *Comte*.

It might be possible to frighten him away from the girl or perhaps to bribe him to leave Baden-Baden and return to Paris.

In the meantime, he told himself, it could be some time before Esmé Seabrooke found another bridegroom.

That would give him time to get in touch with Daniela's family.

Thinking he had found one solution which might work, he slept peacefully until his valet called him.

He usually rode before breakfast in the Black Forest which he found very beautiful and where there were pieces of uncultivated ground on which he could gallop.

It was now, however, he decided, too late to ride before going to the races.

He therefore went down to breakfast.

He was thinking not only about Daniela's problem but also whether or not he should return, as he had intended, to England the next morning.

He had actually told his Valet yesterday that was what he intended to do.

In consequence, he knew that most of his clothes had been packed by Bowles, who had been with him for some years.

He was therefore used to his Master's sudden alteration of plans and his quick decisions.

He would be ready whenever he wished to go.

As the Marquis ate an excellent breakfast he told himself it was impossible that things could be as bad as Daniela had described them last night.

The girl in fact must have been exaggerating.

Bowles had managed to obtain for him English newspapers which were only three days old.

When breakfast was finished the Marquis went into the

very comfortable Study and sat in front of an open window with *The Times* when one of the servants came to the door to say:

"There's a young woman wishing to see you, *Monsieur*. She comes from the Hotel Stephanie and says it is urgent."

The Marquis was instantly alert.

"Show her in."

The maid who came into the room had a woollen shawl over her head.

The Marquis saw at a glance that she was wearing a linen apron over a cotton dress, which told him she was a *femme de chambre*.

"Good morning," he said in German. "You wanted to see me?"

"Yes, *Mein Herr*. A young lady told me to bring you this letter and said you would pay me for doing so. I also, as she said it was urgent, hired a carriage."

"You were quite right," the Marquis said.

He took Daniela's letter, opened it, and read what it contained.

He took three gold louis from his pocket and gave them to the maid, who was almost speechless with delight.

"Thank you, *Mein Herr*, thank you!" she managed to say at last, curtsying as she did so.

She would have gone from the room, but as she turned round the Marquis stopped her.

"Listen," he said, "I want you to go back to the Hotel and pack all *Mademoiselle*'s clothes as quickly as you can."

"Some of them are already packed, *Mein Herr*, and I think perhaps she is going away."

"Pack what is left and see that all her luggage is taken downstairs," the Marquis said.

He paused before continuing:

"If you will do exactly as I tell you without letting anybody know, you will be amply rewarded for your trouble."

"Thank you, *Mein Herr*, thank you!" the maid said again.

Then as she left the room the Marquis sent for Bowles and started giving him his orders.

*   *   *

When Daniela was ready, it was Maria who went into the Sitting-Room to inform her stepmother.

Daniela walked to the window and was looking up at the sky, praying as she did so that the Marquis would be able to save her in time.

She was sensible enough to realise because it was late in the morning that he might already have left the Villa.

However, she knew that the racing in Baden-Baden did not start as early as it did in England.

At the same time, she could not help thinking of dozens of reasons why he should not be at the Villa, in which case he would not get her note until he returned and it would be too late.

"Please, God . . . please . . ."

She felt as if her plea floated up into the sky like a bird.

She could only follow it with every nerve of her body as if she were a part of her own prayer.

Her stepmother came into the bedroom.

"Come on, Daniela!" she said. "What are you mooning about for? André's waiting downstairs in the carriage, and we're all going together."

Daniela knew without her stepmother saying so that this was a precaution in case she should try to run away.

Still, she thought she had to make one last bid for freedom.

"Suppose, Stepmama," she said, "I made over half my fortune to you unconditionally?"

She paused for a moment before she went on:

"Would you then be happy for me to stay with you without having a husband I do not want, and who, as I am well aware belongs to . . . you?"

She thought her suggestion sounded reasonable.

Yet she had known instinctively that her stepmother would treat it with contempt.

Actually Esmé laughed.

"Why should I accept half a loaf," she asked, "when I can have it whole."

There was no answer to this, and she went on:

"Besides, if you do not marry André, another man might not be under an obligation to me, and therefore not so generous."

Her eyes narrowed and her voice sharpened as she said:

"What I'll be having is only what your father promised me. He deceived me by making a Will that tricked me out of what I was entitled to as his wife."

Daniela knew there was no use protesting that her father had never intended to marry her.

The trickery had been on her part to get hold of his money.

'I hate her!' she thought.

She felt her whole being rise in violent revolt against a woman who was so wicked and unscrupulous.

Then with a self-control she had practised ever since she was a child, she knew that nothing would be gained by fighting openly with her stepmother.

She would only feel degraded by indulging in a battle of words.

"Come on!" Esmé was saying. "Your bridegroom is waiting downstairs and I've told the Parson we'd be there by twelve noon!"

There was nothing that Daniela could do but move through the door Maria opened for her and into the passage.

The older *femme de chambre* who had brought in the water for her bath was watching her go, but there was no sign of the younger one.

Daniela could only hope desperately that she had gone, as she had begged her to do, to the Villa d'Horizon.

By now it was ten minutes to twelve.

If the Marquis had been alerted, then in some way, she could not think how, he might manage to spirit her away before the ring was on her finger.

If not, she was the *Comte*'s wife for as long as they lived.

Following her stepmother, Daniela went downstairs into the hall and the Manager of the Hotel came forward to bow and wish her happiness.

She did not reply, but her stepmother said gushingly:

"That's very kind of you, *Monsieur*, and I hope you've arranged the celebration luncheon for when we return."

"Everything is as you ordered, *Madame*," the Manager replied.

They passed out of the door and a carriage was waiting for them.

It was the same one Esmé had used every night to take them to the Casino.

The Protestant Town Church had two high steeples towering above the trees.

Daniela could see it long before the horses drew up outside the West Door.

She had half-hoped as they moved along the narrow roadway that perhaps the Marquis would waylay their carriage.

But there was no sign of him, and as she stepped out she thought he had failed her and now her last hope had gone.

She knew then that she would rather die than be married to the *Comte*.

At least then she would be with her father and mother.

To bear the *Comte*'s name, to know that because they were married she would have to obey him and still live, was an impossibility.

"I must . . . die!" she told herself as she walked up the steps.

She saw as she entered the Church that it was modern and had actually, although she was not aware of it, been in existence only for three years.

It had been built with funds from the Casino.

The *Comte* offered her his arm and they proceeded slowly up the aisle.

Waiting for them in front of the altar was a Clergyman in a white surplice.

He looked very much like the Parson in the Church on her father's estate in England, where she had worshipped every Sunday since she was a small child.

"I am being . . . married," she told herself despairingly.

Even God had failed her.

The *Comte* walked slowly and Daniela could feel vibrations of evil coming from him.

In the quick glance she gave him which she could not prevent herself from making, she saw that he had a smile on his lips.

It was obviously the satisfaction of knowing that in a very few minutes he would be in possession of a very large fortune.

'I must die . . . I must . . . die!' Daniela whispered beneath her breath.

She was aware that her stepmother had followed them up the aisle almost as if she were afraid she would turn and run away at the last moment.

She now moved into the front pew as Daniela and the *Comte* stepped into the Chancel, and were standing in front of the altar.

The Parson, standing a step higher, opened his Prayer Book.

"Dearly beloved . . ." he began, and he was speaking in English.

He was half-way through the first prayer of the Marriage Service when a voice from the back of the Church said loudly:

"Stop this marriage!"

Daniela thought she must be dreaming.

Then, as the *Comte* turned his head instinctively to see who had spoken and the Parson's voice died away, she knew with a leap of her heart that the Marquis was there.

He walked up the aisle, his footsteps ringing out until he reached the Chancel, which was carpeted.

Then, in the same strong, authoritative voice he had used before, he declared:

"This marriage must not take place! The bridegroom is already married, and he has no right to take another wife!"

"Are you sure of this, Sir?" the Parson began.

He was interrupted by the *Comte*, who shouted:

"It's not true! *Ma femme est morte!*"

"That is something that must be proved," the Marquis replied.

It was then that Esmé came from the front pew to stand beside the Marquis.

"What has it got to do with you?" she demanded. "How dare you interfere!"

"I knew the late Lord Seabrooke," the Marquis answered, "and I know he would not want his daughter to become the wife of a Bigamist."

He paused a moment before continuing:

"Or, for that matter, to marry in this 'hole and corner' manner without any of her relatives being present!"

"That's not for you to say, nor for you to interfere!" Esmé replied furiously.

"That is a matter of opinion," the Marquis retorted. "Daniela—go and get into my carriage which is outside waiting."

It was a command.

Daniela, who had been looking at him with shining eyes, picked up the trail of her gown.

Her stepmother came forward to obstruct her, but before she could do so Daniela ran down the aisle quicker than she had ever run in her life.

Through the West Door and down the steps she ran to fling herself into the carriage.

It was standing just behind the one which had brought her with her stepmother and the *Comte* to the Church.

"I'll not allow this!" Esmé Seabrooke screamed as Daniela went.

The Marquis made no reply.

He walked quickly after Daniela, leaving three people staring after him having no idea for the moment of what they could do to stop him.

He too hurried down the steps of the Church and got into the carriage, and a footman shut the door he had been holding open for him.

Immediately the horses moved off.

It was then that Daniela, the tears streaming down her cheeks, turned to him.

"You have ... saved me! Oh ... how could ... you have ... been so ... wonderful! I was ... quite certain ... I would have ... to die!"

chapter five

"You will live," the Marquis replied quietly, "and with any luck without seeing that guttersnipe again!"

When he accused the *Comte* of bigamy, he had been quite certain from the expression in his eyes that it was true and he was aware that his wife was alive.

In that case the Marquis was sure that he would simply disappear and find another way of obtaining money from some unfortunate woman.

At the same time, he was aware that he must save Daniela not only from the *Comte* but—and this was more important—from her stepmother.

He had the idea that Esmé Blanc would not give up easily.

As Cora Pearl had told him, she was determined to have money and he expected she would now resort in some way to blackmail.

Unfortunately, as he had reasoned out on his way to the

Church, she was in a very comfortable position if she was legally Daniela's Guardian.

'If I get the girl to her relations,' the Marquis thought, 'they can sort out all these problems. They are really not my business.'

Then, as he looked at Daniela with her eyes raised to his in gratitude and the tears running down her cheeks, he thought no woman could look more lovely.

"How can . . . I thank . . . you?" she asked in a low voice. "How can I tell . . . you how . . . wonderful you are to have . . . come at the very . . . last minute?"

She gave a little sob as she said:

"As I walked up the aisle I thought even . . . God had . . . forgotten me, but He sent you, I know He did, and now I am . . . safe!"

"We must not count our chickens before they are hatched," the Marquis said quietly. "England is far away, and I am afraid your stepmother will try to prevent you from reaching Seabrooke Hall."

He saw the terror come back into Daniela's eyes and thought it had been a mistake to frighten her.

At the same time, he knew, if he was honest, he was nervous himself that his plans might be circumvented.

He knew both he and Daniela had to be on their guard.

"Do you . . . think," she asked now in a very small, frightened little voice, "that my . . . stepmother will . . . try and . . . stop me at the . . . Station?"

"I am quite certain that is what she will try to do," the Marquis said, "but if she does she will be disappointed."

"Why?" Daniela asked.

"Because we are not leaving Baden-Baden by train!"

Daniela stared at him in astonishment.

"Then . . . how can we . . . get away? We cannot . . . drive all the way to . . . the coast."

"No, of course not," he answered, "but I fortunately have another way of travelling."

Daniela looked at him in perplexity.

As she had been speaking, it had passed through her mind that it would be very difficult to avoid detection.

Everybody would undoubtedly stare at her when she appeared dressed as a bride.

Now, as she wondered what the Marquis was implying, he said with a faint smile:

"As you have already thought, to travel by train or coach is more or less impossible in the circumstances, but there are two other ways you have not mentioned."

"What are they?" Daniela asked.

"Either by balloon, which we do not possess," the Marquis answered, "or by boat, which is actually the way we are going."

Her eyes widened and she repeated:

"By . . . boat?"

For a moment she could not think what he was saying, knowing they were a long way from the sea.

There were mountains all round them, besides the Black Forest which she always thought of as impenetrable.

Then as if he were pleased with himself at having perplexed her, the Marquis said:

"You have forgotten the Rhine!"

Daniela gave a little cry of excitement.

She had in fact learnt a great deal of Geography at the Convent, and was aware that the Rhine was one of the great waterways of Europe.

But it had never struck her that it flowed quite near to Baden-Baden.

"It is only about fourteen miles away," the Marquis said as if he could read her thoughts.

He paused before he went on:

"My friend who lent me the Villa fortunately had this superb team of carriage horses which will make short work of the distance."

Daniela gave a little gasp.

"Then . . . my stepmother can . . . never catch us with the . . . one horse with which we . . . drove to . . . the Church."

"Not unless it had wings!" the Marquis smiled.

"How could you . . . think of . . . anything so . . . clever, so marvelous?" Daniela asked.

She clasped her hands together as she spoke and looked so radiant that the Marquis felt as if the sunshine had suddenly lit the inside of the carriage.

As they drove out of the old town of Baden-Baden with its seventeenth-century houses, Daniela felt as if they were flying into the sky.

She was leaving her problems and fears behind her.

They had driven for some distance before she said a little hesitatingly:

"There is . . . only one other problem . . . and I hate to . . . bother you with it."

"What is that?" the Marquis asked.

"I . . . I have . . . nothing to wear . . . aboard ship but this wedding-gown!"

She thought as she spoke that because her stepmother had chosen it for her for the Wedding Service, she never wanted to see it again.

"Are you under-estimating my powers of organisation?" the Marquis asked with a note of amusement in his voice.

"It is something on which I pride myself, and now I consider you are insulting me."

"How could I . . . ever do such . . . a thing as . . . that?" Daniela asked quickly. "At the . . . same time . . ."

She paused.

"I think you will find," the Marquis said, "unless something has gone very wrong and the maid you sent with the note has not carried out my instructions, that your luggage will be waiting for you on board the *Sea Horse*."

Daniela stared at him in disbelief.

"My yacht will be ready for us when we get to the Rhine," he continued, "and your luggage is now travelling ahead in a Brake drawn by six horses."

"I do not . . . believe it!" Daniela said. "I am . . . dreaming, for no one except . . . a Magician could be as . . . fantastic as . . . you."

"Thank you," the Marquis said. "I only hope you will not be disappointed and the six horses will not turn into mice and the Brake into a pumpkin!"

Daniela laughed as he meant her to do, and leant back against the comfortable padded seat.

"Only a . . . Magician," she said softly, "could have a yacht . . . waiting for him at . . . exactly the moment it was . . . most needed."

The Marquis knew himself it was really a lucky chance, since if there was one thing he hated, it was travelling by train.

The railway might be a recent innovation, but he found trains noisy and uncomfortable.

He disliked being rattled along at what he thought was too quick a speed, and he also disliked being unable to spend the night in a comfortable bed.

In England when he was going on a long journey he

invariably had his own private carriage attached to a train.

Because he was of such importance, there was no difficulty about it.

When he decided to come from Paris to Baden-Baden, there had been endless formalities.

The private carriage he hired was not in any way as comfortable as his own, and he had found the whole journey extremely disagreeable.

Anticipating this before he left Paris, he had sent a message to the Captain of his yacht, which was in harbour at Calais.

He ordered him to proceed up the Rhine and dock as near as possible to Baden-Baden.

He knew the *Sea Horse* would enter the Rhine through Holland.

As it was a wide river, if the Captain steamed at full speed the journey would not take more than a few days.

There it would remain until he required it.

He knew that unless something very radical had gone wrong, the *Sea Horse* would now be there.

It was something that Esmé Seabrooke would not anticipate.

It would take her undoubtedly some time to discover in which direction Daniela had vanished.

The Marquis could not help feeling that it must have been his remarkable perception that had warned him that the *Sea Horse* should be available at exactly the right spot.

If he had still been eager to be with Cora Pearl, he might have returned with her to Paris.

As it was, he found time while the carriage was being brought round with its team of four horses to scribble her a note.

He told her he unfortunately had to leave for England unexpectedly without saying goodbye.

He thanked her for the happy time they had spent together.

He enclosed a present which he hoped she would like and which when she wore it would bring back memories of the occasion.

Hastily he gave the note with the small parcel to the Major Domo in charge of his friend's Villa.

He thought now that the present he had bought for Cora Pearl could not be more appropriate.

Again he wondered if his perception was not almost clair-voyant.

He had seen in the shop of Oscar Massin, who was un-doubtedly the most celebrated and most original Jeweller in Paris, a necklace of black pearls.

The Marquis had gone in expecting to buy one of the magnificent jewels by which Massin had become famous.

His diamond bouquets and foliage had been acclaimed as the finest work of the century.

The Marquis was actually considering whether he would give Cora Pearl a spray of eglantine and lilies-of-the-valley, which seemed to shine with an iridescent light.

Then he had seen the necklace of black pearls.

He thought it was something Cora did not possess.

It would look sensational against her white skin, which was one of the most acclaimed elements in her beauty.

What he had not expected was the black jet bed in which he had made love to her last night.

He thought now with a twist of his lips that she would wear it for her next lover.

He would doubtless be enthralled by the picture she would make, naked against the black background, the pearls round her long neck.

Then he told himself it was a fitting end to a chapter.

Even when he returned to Paris he would not be with Cora Pearl again.

The Marquis liked variety in the women on whom he bestowed his favours for the simple reason that his interest in them was entirely physical.

He found they had little to offer him apart from their bodies.

When he wanted to talk of things that interested him, he talked with a man.

Women to him were just flowers he liked to see about him, and when a flower withered, it was easily replaced by another.

Now that he thought of it, he had never taken so much trouble over any woman as he had over Daniela.

He supposed it was because she was English and he had to behave like a Gentleman.

He had rescued her from an intolerable position in which she found herself through no fault of her own.

At the same time, he was certain that once they were aboard the *Sea Horse* he would find himself yawning until they reached England.

He had to congratulate himself, however, that he had been clever in preventing the marriage, spiriting her away without causing too much commotion, except for Esmé Seabrooke screaming at him.

He could not help wondering what had happened after he had left.

He thought the Clergyman would certainly demand an enquiry into the *Comte*'s background, which would ensure that he would vanish as quickly as possible.

"It is all really quite amusing," the Marquis told himself.

He found himself regretting he would not see his second

horse run in the races this afternoon, as he had intended to do.

Both his horses would tomorrow start on a long journey by train until they reached Newmarket, where his stables lay.

Out in the open and away from the trees that were part of the Black Forest the carriage was moving very swiftly.

There was an expression of rapture on Daniela's face.

As the Marquis glanced at her, he knew that she was saying a prayer of gratitude to God for her escape.

He thought it very touching.

It was something which he had never known any other woman of his acquaintance to do however fortunate she might have been either in love or at the card-table.

To be certain he was not mistaken, he said:

"I may be wrong, but I have the feeling you are saying a prayer for your escape."

Daniela turned to look at him, her eyes very large in her small face.

"Last . . . night," she replied, "I felt my . . . prayers were . . . going up to . . . God like birds . . . flying into the . . . sky. I felt too . . . as if I . . . flew with . . . them."

"And God has helped you."

"He . . . sent you to . . . save me," Daniela said simply, "and I feel that . . . Papa and Mama had . . . a hand in it too . . . in fact, I have a great many prayers to say."

Then, as if she thought the Marquis was slightly sceptical, although she had no idea why he should feel like that, she added:

"Papa always said that people were very ungrateful. They whined and complained when things went wrong, but never remembered to thank God when they went right."

"I suppose that is true," the Marquis agreed.

"They thank for presents," Daniela went on, following her train of thought, "but when I was a little girl, Mama used to make me count my blessings."

"I am sure you had a great number of them," the Marquis remarked.

"I was not thinking of toys and parties, and the pony I used to ride," Daniela answered. "Mama taught me to thank for my eyes and my ears, my fingers and my toes, and also for my brain."

"Your brain?" the Marquis repeated in surprise.

"That is certainly something you should be grateful for," Daniela said. "Although I was pleading to your heart to take compassion . . . on me, it was your brain which made you clever enough to rescue me at the last moment, and it is your brain which is taking us now to join your yacht."

She paused before she went on:

"It will be like the dolphin which guided Apollo to the port in Greece beneath the Shining Cliffs."

There was a rapt expression on her face as she spoke which told the Marquis that, as a number of other women had, she was comparing him to Apollo.

He had, however, forgotten about the dolphin, and he thought it was rather clever of Daniela to make the comparison.

"I can understand," she was saying, "why you called your yacht the *Sea Horse* but perhaps the *Sea Dolphin* would have been a better name."

"I do not believe a dolphin would have been as swift," the Marquis said.

"I suppose that is true," Daniela replied, "and I am very, very grateful for a horse that can gallop on water and carry me down the Rhine, home to England."

A little later the Marquis felt that the horses which had

brought them quicker than he would have believed possible to the Rhine should be congratulated.

Without his saying anything, when Daniela climbed out of the carriage, she went to pat each one of them.

She had discarded her wedding-veil and thrown it on the floor and added the wreath of orange blossom which she thought she never wanted to see again.

In fact, she said as she took it from her hair:

"If I ever marry . . . which I think unlikely, I will never . . . never wear a . . . wreath of . . . orange blossom!"

"Why should you not marry?" the Marquis asked curiously, thinking it was a strange remark for a young girl to make.

"I was thinking last night," Daniela said, "it would be impossible to find someone who loved me for myself."

The Marquis thought that was a ridiculous statement, seeing how lovely she was, but she went on:

"Papa always longed to have a son, and I remember once when I was about ten hearing Mama say when she did not know I was listening:

"'Oh, darling, if only I could have given you a son to inherit this house and all the treasures you and your ancestors have collected, you would have been very proud of me.'"

She remembered as she spoke how her father had put his arms round her and said:

"You are not to worry about it, my precious. We have Daniela, who is very like you, and what man could want more than to own two such very beautiful women?"

For a moment her mother had just lain her cheek against her father's and said:

"As you well know, it is a great mistake for a girl to be rich. There will be fortune-hunters clustering round her, while the decent men will keep away because no man likes to have a wife richer than himself.''

Lord Seabrooke laughed, then he said:

''I am prepared to bet a considerable amount of money that if Daniela is as beautiful as you, a man will not worry as to whether she has a fortune, or only a penny to her name.''

He had kissed his wife on the cheek.

''He will lose his heart irretrievably, as I have done, and then nothing else matters!''

As Daniela was telling the Marquis what she had heard, she was looking out of the window.

''Perhaps I shall be lucky like Mama,'' she said, ''but I have a feeling there are a great number of . . . men like . . . the *Comte* and once I am married . . . you will not be there to . . . help me . . . escape.''

''It does present a problem,'' the Marquis answered quietly. ''At the same time, you are very young, Daniela, and you will find after you have been presented at Court by your grandmother and have attended a number of Balls, you will meet a great many Englishmen who are much richer than you are.''

He paused to smile at her before continuing:

''You will therefore not be concerned with anything but your face, and, of course, your heart.''

Daniela did not reply and he had the feeling she did not believe him.

When she had patted the horses and thanked the coachman for the speed they had achieved, she turned to look excitedly at the Marquis.

He was already beginning to walk to where moored close to the riverside she could see the *Sea Horse*.

Daniela saw as she followed him that a little farther on

under the shade of some trees there was a Brake.

It was drawn by six horses and it had, as the Marquis predicted, arrived before them.

"Everything has happened just as you meant it to," she said as she followed him to the gangway. "How can you be so . . . clever?"

"I am pleased my orders have been carried out," the Marquis said. "I should in fact have been not only annoyed but also humiliated if anything had gone wrong."

The way he spoke was so positive that Daniela knew it was the truth.

She walked up the gangplank to where she could see the Captain of the yacht waiting for them, and the Marquis introduced them.

She shook hands, then a steward opened a door of the superstructure which she found led into the Saloon.

It was then she heard the Marquis say:

"I wish to leave immediately, Captain, with the greatest speed of which we are capable!"

"Very good, My Lord," the Captain replied.

The Marquis just had time to tip the coachman of the Brake before the gangplank was pulled aboard and the *Sea Horse* began to move downstream.

Daniela was looking round the Saloon, which was decorated in green and hung with sporting pictures which she guessed came from the Marquis's collection.

As she felt the engines accelerate she ran to the glass windows on both sides of the Saloon to look out at the shores they were passing.

"We have Germany on one side of us," she said to the Marquis, "and France on the other!"

"That is exactly what I was going to tell you," he replied, "but I can see you are well informed."

"I am trying to remember the Legends I have heard about the Rhine," she said, "but I am sure, as you will know them better than I do, you will be able to tell me about them."

The Marquis thought this was something he had never been asked before.

He usually thought it a bore to take women with him to sea.

They were invariably sea-sick, and because they felt they had him to themselves and there were few other distractions, they were too demanding.

This meant that they only wanted him to make love to them and they were interested in nothing except themselves.

He remembered that last year he had made a mistake in taking a very pretty woman with a small party of friends up the Seine to Paris.

He knew long before they had reached the gayest Capital in Europe he had made a great mistake in bringing, as he said to himself, "coals to Newcastle."

He had thought the journey would be amusing as they stopped at various places *en voyage* and ate at French Restaurants where the food was superlative.

But the woman he had with him was slimming in order to retain her eighteen-inch waist.

She therefore merely pecked at the delicious *pâté de canard* and refused the dishes that could be produced only by a French Chef.

By the time they reached Paris the Marquis was inevitably bored.

He sent his party back by train without accompanying them and had vowed to himself: 'Never again!'

The stewards began to bring in the luncheon, and as Daniela looked at it she said to the Marquis:

"May I wait to change until after luncheon? I am very hungry!"

"You look very attractive just as you are," the Marquis said automatically as he would have said to any other woman he was with.

Daniela, however, laughed.

"You know that nothing could be more unsuitable on a yacht than a Bridal gown!" she said. "But as there is no one to impress except the fishes, I am sure you will forgive me for making a social gaffe!"

The Marquis laughed.

"Let us have a glass of champagne. We have a great deal to celebrate, but you must not drink too much until you have had something to eat."

He remembered how frightened she had been last night and was sure she had eaten very little dinner.

He also suspected she had been too terrified to have any breakfast.

"I will be very careful," Daniela answered, "and although I would like to sip a little champagne, as you say, to celebrate, I would much rather drink lemonade or water."

As they sat down at the table she took large helpings of every course that was served and praised what she ate in a way that told the Marquis she had an unexpected knowledge of food.

He did not comment on this until she remarked that the dish they were then eating was so good because of the truffles in it.

"It is very difficult to get truffles in England," she said, "in fact, usually it is impossible. But in some dishes, especially this one, they make all the difference."

"How do you know so much about French food?" the

Marquis asked. "I cannot believe they employed a Chef at the Convent."

Daniela laughed.

"No, indeed! We had very simple fare which, it was said, was good for our souls! But Papa always loved *haute cuisine* and Mama became an expert in choosing what he enjoyed. In fact, when we sometimes had a French Chef, she would teach him rather than let him teach us!"

"Are you telling me that you can cook too?" the Marquis asked.

"Not as well as Mama, but I am quite good," Daniela said. "One day, if you will let me, I will cook all the dishes which were Papa's favourites."

It struck the Marquis that it would be rather amusing to take her to some of the places in Paris where the food was considered superb.

They were where the Chefs vied to defeat each other like boxers in a ring.

It made him think of a remark a friend had made when he was last in Paris.

"In this country you can seduce a man's wife," he said, "and steal his mistress, but entice away his Chef and he will shoot you through the heart!"

The Marquis had laughed at the time.

He thought now that only in France could he find the very high standard of cuisine which he himself enjoyed.

He had found in most English houses that the food was well cooked, edible, but lacking in imagination.

However, in his own houses, and especially at Crowle, he took immense trouble over the menus.

But they were invariably fully appreciated only by his male guests.

They talked about the food of different countries for quite

a long time, in fact, until the luncheon was finished.

Then Daniela said:

"Please, I am longing to explore the yacht, and could I speak to your Chef and tell him how much I have enjoyed this delicious meal?"

"Yes, of course," the Marquis answered, "but I think perhaps you should change first."

She looked down at her gown as she spoke.

He knew she had actually forgotten that she was wearing a Bridal gown.

"Yes, of course I must change," she said quickly. "But is it really true, Mister Magician, that my own clothes are below?"

"Unless some Siren from the Rhine has magicked them out of the port-hole, that is where they will be," the Marquis replied.

Daniela jumped up from the table like a child.

"I will go to look for myself, but I am quite certain none of this is real . . . the yacht . . . the luncheon . . . or you!"

As she reached the Saloon door she looked back to say:

"I am sure I shall wake up to find this is all a dream!"

Then she was gone, and the Marquis, who had meant to escort her below, thought she was very different from any other woman who had been aboard the *Sea Horse*.

"She is only a child," he told himself, "and it will be a pity when she grows up and becomes self-conscious and is very demanding of every man who is attracted by her."

Then he thought, as he had when he was talking about her being presented at Court and going to Balls, that it was not going to be easy!

How could it be with Esmé insisting that she was her Guardian?

When he thought it over carefully, he was certain that

now, having been defeated in marrying Daniela off to her lover, Esmé would be planning to come to England.

She could move in to Seabrooke Hall.

The Marquis began to wonder who among Daniela's relations would be strong enough to cope with her.

It would certainly need a man as ruthless and determined as himself.

He wondered if he could somehow frighten Esmé away.

Alternatively, he could bribe her to live in Paris, or take her to Court for illegally exploiting her stepdaughter in attempting to marry her to a Bigamist.

He knew this last solution was extremely undesirable, for it would mean a scandal.

The inevitable publicity in the newspapers would undoubtedly harm Daniela's reputation.

That meant one of the other solutions must be tried in some form or other before anything more serious was considered.

The difficulty was to find someone strong enough to cope with a woman who was completely unscrupulous.

Esmé was concerned only with grasping every penny she could of Daniela's fortune.

"I will talk to Daniela tonight and find out what relatives she has," the Marquis told himself.

At the same time, he was uncomfortably aware that while he had known Lord Seabrooke, he could not think of any other male members of the family he had encountered either on the race-course or at Whites.

"There must be someone!" he reassured himself confidently.

But he could not help feeling doubtful.

                              *   *   *

In an incredibly short time, Daniela came running up the
companionway and into the Saloon.

She was now dressed in a pretty, simple gown, which
any young girl might have worn in the garden or on un-
important occasions.

Because her figure was so good, in fact the Marquis could
not help thinking as good, if not better than Cora Pearl's,
she looked very alluring.

Her eyes were shining, her lips were smiling.

She seemed part of the fairy-story in which she believed
she was taking part.

"I have been very quick," she said, "because your kind
Valet had already unpacked my clothes. He is such a nice
man!"

"That is what I have always found myself," the Marquis
replied, "but you are not to encourage him to gossip."

"Why not?" Daniela enquired.

"Because he talks too much and knows too much!" the
Marquis answered.

It was the sort of remark which would make his usual
guests scream with laughter.

"You mean he knows too much about you?" Daniela
asked. "Papa always said that no man could be a hero to
his Valet."

"As far as I am concerned," the Marquis said, "without
being conceited, I think Bowles makes me out to be too
much of a hero. In fact, he turns my escapades into vic-
tories."

"Which I expect is what they are!" Daniela replied.

"And as you are a hero to me, Bowles and I will get along very well together."

She spoke without giving him a coquettish glance.

Nor was she flirtatious in the sort of way which the Marquis had always found inevitable whenever a woman talked about him personally.

Instead, she stated it just as a fact. Then before he could reply she said:

"Oh, please, let me see the yacht, and I want to inspect the engines, which sound just like the buzz of the bees."

Good-humouredly and because he was very proud of the *Sea Horse*, a great deal of which he had designed himself, the Marquis took her on a tour of inspection.

To his surprise, she talked intelligently about everything, and asked questions which occasionally he had to refer to the Captain.

She was wildly enthusiastic about all the gadgets, most of which the Marquis knew were different from what was found on most yachts, and which he had insisted on being installed.

She was thrilled by the Galley.

She left the Chef beaming with satisfaction when she talked to him about his food, making it obvious to him that she had a special knowledge of it.

"I'll cook you something really special for dinner, *M'mselle*."

"I shall look forward to it," Daniela answered, "and I will not waste a mouthful."

The Chef had laughed at that.

"Most of the ladies M'Lord has had aboard," he said, "are so worried about their figures that they do not eat enough to keep a mouse alive!"

"Well, I am the exception," Daniela replied, "and as I

am greedy, please let the menu be a long one."

"Now you have offered him a challenge," the Marquis said as they walked away from the Galley. "We shall, if we are not careful, be eating until midnight!"

"And enjoying ourselves," Daniela exclaimed.

The Marquis thought that most women would have said, rather, that they were enjoying themselves with him and nothing else was of importance.

Again he told himself that Daniela was very young. In a few years she would not be interested in food, but only in the compliments she would receive from some besotted man.

They inspected every inch of the yacht from the bow to the stern.

Daniela eulogised over the engines.

Then they sank down in two deck-chairs which had been arranged for them under an awning on the shady side of the deck.

They were very comfortable chairs made of basket-work with a stool on which they could rest their feet.

Daniela leaned back against soft cushions.

"This is lovely!" she said ecstatically. "As you are too young to want to go to sleep, will you tell me some of the Legends of the Rhine?"

The Marquis looked at her in surprise.

"Are you really interested in the Legends?" he asked.

"Of course!" she answered. "Although I know a little about Lohengrin, the Knight of the Swan, I would like to hear you tell me about him, and, of course, about Brunhilde, Hagen, and Siegfried, whose sword decapitated him."

The Marquis held up his hands in horror.

"I will give you a book of all the Legends," he said. "It

is a long time since I was at school, and I am afraid I have forgotten them."

Daniela thought for a moment, then she said in a small voice:

"I think . . . the truth is . . . you are finding me . . . rather a bore . . . and I am . . . sorry. If you want just to think . . . I will be . . . very quiet and not . . . disturb you."

The Marquis smiled.

"We have not been acquainted very long, Daniela, and so far you have certainly not been a bore. In fact, everything about you has been dramatic and, when you look back, exciting."

"It was the most frightening thing that had ever happened to me, until I heard your voice behind me in the Church," Daniela said in a low tone. "I had been . . . trying to . . . think how I could . . . die before I had to be . . . alone with the *Comte* . . . then suddenly . . . you were there!"

It was impossible, the Marquis thought, not to find the sudden lilt in her voice very moving.

"This morning," Daniela went on as if she were looking back on it all, "before we entered the Church, I offered my stepmother half my fortune if I did not have to . . . marry the *Comte*. I said I would be happy to stay with her if I did not have a . . . husband I did not . . . want . . . and—"

Daniela paused for a moment, then as if she forced herself she finished:

"—and who . . . belonged to her!"

The Marquis knew that she was once again shocked.

She was appalled that the *Comte* should try to marry her at the same time as he was making love to her stepmother.

Because he thought it was a mistake to encourage her to be introspective, he asked quickly:

"What did your stepmother reply?"

"She said: 'Why should I accept half a loaf when I can have the whole?' "

"Forget her!" the Marquis said sharply. "At least for the moment."

Then as he realised that was really not possible, he went on:

"You said that this yacht is magical and I am a Magician."

He smiled at her before continuing:

"You have to trust me, therefore, to get you out of the difficulties that lie ahead, just as I have spirited you away from the one you were facing this morning."

"You certainly . . . did that," Daniela said, "and it was so wonderful . . . wonderful of you . . . that I still . . . cannot believe . . . that it is . . . true!"

"It is true," the Marquis said, "and at least for the moment you are safe on the *Sea Horse*. Because I want you to be happy, I suggest you try to forget your stepmother and concentrate on enjoying yourself."

"I am sure I can do that by . . . eating your . . . delicious food," Daniela said, "and thinking how . . . beautiful the . . . Rhine is!"

The Marquis's eyes twinkled.

He knew that was not the answer any other woman would have given him.

Even Cora Pearl would have made the automatic response that was expected of her.

There was silence for a moment. Then Daniela said:

"You are . . . right, because if one . . . thinks of one's . . . enemies it gives them a . . . power over you. We must think only very beautiful and happy thoughts, and then nothing that is evil can come near us."

The Marquis thought she was making it all into a fairy-story.

He could only pray that unlike in many of the Legends of the Rhine there would be a happy ending.

"That is exactly what we will do," he said, "and, of course, as the only Lady aboard, you have to amuse me and think of ways to prevent me from becoming bored."

Daniela laughed.

"Now you are . . . talking like . . . a Sultan: 'Bring on the Dancing-Girls!' "

"They are in rather short supply," the Marquis answered.

"Now you are not using your imagination," Daniela replied. "You have to multiply me by five or perhaps more, and I will do my best to oblige!"

She made a little obeisance with her hands as she spoke which the Marquis thought was very graceful.

Then she asked:

"Is it true that at a party in Paris the Prince Napoleon offered Cora Pearl, who was with you last night, a whole van-load of the most expensive orchids?"

The Marquis frowned as she spoke, but Daniela did not notice as she went on:

"She gave a supper-party, the orchids were strewn all over the floor, and dressed as a sailor she danced a Hornpipe, followed by the Can-Can over them."

"Who has been telling you these stories?" the Marquis asked, not wishing to admit it was true.

"My stepmother talked about it when she was fitting on two orchids she had bought to wear with her gown last night," Daniela replied.

Then she put her fingers to her lips in dismay.

"I . . . I am sorry . . . I have mentioned . . . her and it is . . . something you told me . . . not to do!"

"I told you to forget her," the Marquis said sharply, "and you are also to forget Cora Pearl and all the women like her. Once you are out of this mess, Daniela, you will have to understand that you are a Lady!"

Daniela made a little murmur, but he went on:

"Ladies know nothing about the women of Paris who were at the Casino last night, or someone like your step-mother who tries to emulate them."

"I am . . . sorry," Daniela said in a contrite little voice, "but I thought you liked . . . women like . . . them and Papa must have liked Madame Blanc . . . until she married him."

She gave a little sigh.

"But . . . I shall never be . . . like them."

"Thank God for that!" the Marquis exclaimed sharply. "Do you not understand, you stupid child, that you are different? Your loveliness is not put on with a paint-brush, and you do not have to dance on orchids to attract a man. You are what a man wants as a wife, and not in any other capacity."

He spoke harshly and Daniela sat thinking it over. Then she said:

"Are you . . . telling me that despite my . . . money . . . a man who is really nice and a gentleman like you . . . and Papa . . . might want to . . . marry me just . . . because I am . . . me?"

"Of course that is what I am saying," the Marquis said. "A man will love you because you are not only a very beautiful person, but also good and pure."

Then, as he saw Daniela's eyes light up and an expression on her face which was very revealing, he thought he was on dangerous ground.

In fact, from his point of view—very dangerous.

chapter six

"Look! Look! I have never seen anything so beautiful! It is enchanting! It is Fairyland!"

Because Daniela was so excited and thrilled, the Marquis found that he, too, was moved by the beauty of the river.

When they reached Bingen, he agreed as they steamed on to Koblenz that it was, as Daniela thought, a Fairyland.

There was Castle after Castle on either side of them and one lovely vista after another appearing ahead.

It was difficult for Daniela to know which view-point on the yacht was the best.

She ran up and down the deck, frightened she would miss something.

Because she was so enthusiastic, the Marquis found himself remembering stories which he had not thought of since he was a boy.

He pointed out Lahneck, the stronghold of the Knights

Templars, and the King's seat at Königsstuhl, where the Emperors used to be elected.

When there were no Castles, cascades, or cliffs to admire, there were barges moving up and down the river which Daniela also found enthralling.

Some of them were carrying coal and coke destined for Italy, others Russian petrol and Prussian wheat.

A number, as the Marquis pointed out, were bringing timber from the Black Forest.

It was difficult for him to persuade Daniela to come into the Saloon for luncheon because she was determined not to miss anything.

He found himself thinking he had never in the past known a woman so excited by nature.

She plied him with questions.

He was reluctant to have to admit that he was ignorant about much she wished to know.

She longed to stop at Woerth, where below the falls there was a medieval Castle.

It stood in the middle of the river and could be reached only by a footbridge, where both banks of the river were thick with larches, pines, and oak-trees.

"Please let us just go and look at it," Daniela pleaded.

The Marquis shook his head.

"It would be a mistake not to get to England as quickly as possible."

Now that he had reminded her that her stepmother might be pursuing them, it was in a very different tone of voice that she said:

"Yes . . . yes . . . of course. You are right . . . as you always . . . are!"

Although he told himself it was unnecessary, the Marquis was worried.

Esmé might be taking steps to get hold of Daniela before he could deliver her safely to her relatives.

He therefore told the Captain that no member of the crew was to mention to anybody outside the yacht that he had a guest with him.

"If anybody asks questions, I am travelling alone. Make it known that any man who disobeys my order will be dismissed immediately!"

The Captain was surprised at the way the Marquis spoke, but he said quietly:

"I assure you, My Lord, your orders will be carried out by every man aboard the *Sea Horse*."

The second evening after they had come aboard Daniela and the Marquis went out on deck.

They had finished what once again was a delicious and unusual dinner.

The last glimmer of crimson in the sky showed where the sun had set.

The stars were already beginning to glitter overhead.

The banks of the river had become mysterious and even more romantic than they had been in the daytime.

Now it was hard not to believe in the legend of the Niebelungen treasure and the lovely lady who lured the fishermen to their doom.

Heine and Liszt had made it famous, but seeing the steep creeper-covered rock standing sheer in the water made it real.

Watching Daniela's face in the fading light, the Marquis thought she was re-living everything she had ever learnt or he had told her.

For the moment the Rhine was peopled not with barges and ships, but with the nymphs that swam in its shallow waters.

Knights in their Shining Armour patrolled the Castles.

The gods used their power to sweep away the evil of those who were always plotting against what was good and noble.

They did not speak for a long time.

They leant on the railing and looked ahead until Daniela said with a little sigh:

"It is so beautiful that it makes me feel as I . . . sometimes do . . . in Church."

"And how do you feel then?" the Marquis asked.

"As if my heart were being . . . carried up to the sky and my . . . prayers were part of the . . . music the angels . . . sing."

Her voice was very soft, as if she were speaking to herself.

Then she said:

"Now this loveliness is a . . . part of me . . . and I shall . . . never be . . . able to . . . forget it."

She threw back her head as she spoke to look up at the stars above.

The Marquis felt as if she, too, were part of the angels she heard singing.

"She is lovely—too lovely to be left alone with nobody to look after her," he told himself.

For the first time an idea occurred to him!

It would be thought reprehensible and would certainly damage her reputation if it became known that she was travelling alone with him in his yacht.

He knew exactly what construction would be put upon it.

Not only by the Dowagers in the Social World of Mayfair, but also by the members of his Clubs.

He knew, however, that it had not entered Daniela's mind that she ought to have a Chaperone.

She had not shown in any way that she was embarrassed at being alone with him.

He knew it was her innocence and her ignorance of the Social World that made her behave as naturally as if he were her father or her brother.

It was, he told himself with a faint smile, very good for his ego.

He was so used to being flattered and pursued by every woman he met.

It was an entirely new experience to find himself more of a Tutor than a lover.

He knew that Daniela was comparing him, because he had saved her, with the Knights who had fought so valiantly on the banks of the Rhine.

Alternatively, she identified him with one of the gods who had directed and inspired them.

They were still believed in by the peasants.

Dusk had turned into darkness and the stars shone more brilliantly than diamonds.

Finally he drew Daniela back into the Saloon.

"I cannot . . . bear to leave . . . it," she protested.

"It will be there tomorrow," the Marquis said, "although after we pass Cologne, the Rhine will not be as beautiful as it is here."

There was silence.

Then she said a little wistfully:

"I . . . I suppose we could . . . not stop at Cologne, which I know is called 'the Rome of the North' and see the . . . Cathedral?"

She gave a little sigh as she continued:

"I learned about it at School with the Nuns. It is the fifth largest in the world, and took 632 years to build!"

The Marquis smiled.

"I think it would be a mistake on this voyage, but you will be able to come back another time."

"That . . . might be . . . impossible," Daniela said almost beneath her breath.

The Marquis could see by the expression on her face that she was thinking that her stepmother might then be in charge of her.

Esmé would certainly be more interested in Casinos than Cathedrals.

To change the subject, he said:

"What I must do is try to buy you a bottle of Eau de Cologne. It was invented in 1709 when it was discovered that pure spirit combined with orange-blossom formed an excellent basis for an alluring scent."

He was speaking to divert Daniela's mind from her stepmother.

He realised only when he had said the words "orange-blossom" that he had made a mistake.

Daniela jumped to her feet and went to the open window to look out into the darkness.

There were little flickering lights on the shore, some of which appeared to be climbing up the cliffs by themselves until they finally reached the top.

Then she could see the tips of mountains silhouetted against the sky.

For a moment she did not speak.

"Suppose . . . when she comes to England . . . ." she said, "my stepmother produces another man whom she . . . wishes me to marry? How can I . . . find you?"

The Marquis knew her question was very important, and after a moment he replied:

"I promise you will always know where to get in touch with me. But I intend to be certain you have one of your relatives to take care of you and prevent that sort of thing from happening again.''

Daniela did not reply, and after a moment he said:

''You have been so busy admiring the Rhine that I have had no time to talk to you about which of your relatives we can go to for help.''

''I cannot . . . think of . . . anyone,'' Daniela replied.

''But there must be someone!'' the Marquis insisted. ''Did your father have no brothers?''

''One . . . but he is dead.''

''And your mother?''

''My grandfather—Mama's father—is very old, in fact, he is over eighty! His only son was killed in India five years ago.''

The Marquis was silent, and Daniela went on:

''I think that the fact that I had almost no male relations is the reason why Papa made his Solicitors my Trustees.''

She paused a moment and then continued:

''He always said he did not think women were good at business.''

''There I agree with him,'' the Marquis said.

At the same time, he was thinking it would be very difficult for Daniela to oppose Esmé Blanc's contention that she was her natural Guardian.

However, he did not want Daniela to lie awake worrying over it, so he said lightly:

''There is no hurry. We will talk about it later, perhaps when we are in the North Sea and have to divert our minds from feeling sea-sick.''

''Are you afraid that is what I shall be?'' Daniela asked. ''Bowles told me that you dislike having women on board because they are sick in a rough sea, and do not really fit into a yacht, even as luxurious as this one.''

"Bowles talks too much," the Marquis answered. "But there is some truth in that."

"I promise you I will not be sea-sick."

She paused, then she added:

"I shall only be . . . frightened and upset that our . . . enchanted journey is coming . . . to an end . . . and you will be . . . glad to be rid of me."

"I have not said that," the Marquis answered.

"But I am sure you are thinking it," Daniela persisted, "and I am very conscious that I am an . . . encumbrance."

"Now you are fishing for compliments," the Marquis remarked. "In fact, I have enjoyed our conversations today."

"And I have loved every . . . moment of them," Daniela said in a rapt little voice. "You have made everything seem so real, and as soon as I get back to England, I am going to read everything that Heine wrote about the Rhine, and play everything that Liszt and Beethoven composed about it."

She smiled and went on:

"Of course I must find a book with all the Legends you have told me, and I expect there are a great many more."

"There are," the Marquis agreed, "but now I am thinking up those I can tell you tomorrow, so you had better go to bed and wait until it is light enough for you to see what particular Castle is on either side of us."

"You are . . . so kind to . . . me," Daniela said.

She came back from the window, and as she did so he rose from the chair in which he had been sitting.

"Goodnight, Daniela," he said, "and sleep well. The spirits of the Rhine will be watching over you."

"And . . . so will you," Daniela said softly, almost beneath her breath.

The Marquis put out his hand, meaning to touch her on the shoulder as she dropped him a little curtsy.

Instead, she took his hand in both of hers and kissed it.

He felt the soft touch of her lips against his skin.

Then, as if she were shy, she turned and disappeared from the saloon as swiftly as if she had wings.

The Marquis stood listening to her footsteps going down the companionway.

Then with a frown between his eyes he walked out on deck.

* * *

The Marquis was fast asleep.

He had not gone to bed for several hours after Daniela had left him.

Now he heard Bowles say in a low voice:

"Wake up, M'Lord!"

The Marquis opened his eyes.

His Valet was standing just inside the door.

He knew without looking at the clock that it was earlier than the time he had ordered Bowles to call him.

"What is it?" he asked.

The Valet came nearer to the bed.

"A member of the River Police, M'Lord, has told the Captain we're not to pass Cologne, but dock in the harbour!"

The Marquis sat up in bed.

"For what reason?" he asked sharply.

"I understands, M'Lord, the Chief of Police wants the *Sea 'Orse* searched for a missin' person!"

The Marquis drew in his breath. Then he said:

"Tell the Policeman who is aboard that I will be delighted

to see him as soon as I am dressed. In the meantime, order him a good breakfast in the Saloon, then come back to me.''

''Very good, M'Lord.''

Bowles left the cabin, and the Marquis, slipping on his dressing-gown, went quickly to Daniela's cabin, which was next to his.

He opened the door without knocking and went in.

She was fast asleep.

As he walked towards her he saw that she had drawn back the curtains over the port-holes.

He knew it was because she wanted to look out at the stars before she fell asleep.

Now a pale sun was gently sweeping away the mists over the river.

The light seemed to linger on Daniela's fair hair where it lay spread over her pillow.

Her eye-lashes were dark against the clarity of her skin.

Looking down at her, the Marquis thought it was impossible for any woman to look more beautiful.

Because it had been so hot during the night, she had thrown aside the linen sheet which was all that had covered her.

He could see, through the fine lawn of her nightgown which was trimmed with lace, the perfect curves of her breasts and the outline of her hip.

It flashed through his mind that it would be very exciting if he woke her with a kiss.

He wanted to find out with his lips if hers were as soft as they had been when she kissed his hand.

''Daniela, wake up!'' he said with an effort.

There was a faint smile on her lips as if his voice were part of her dreams.

''Wake up!'' he said again.

Now her long eye-lashes flickered and her eyes opened.

There was an incredible gladness because he was there and he said quickly:

"There is danger. A member of the River Police has come aboard, and you have to hide!"

"M-my . . . stepmother?"

The word seemed to burst from her lips as Daniela sat up in bed.

"I am afraid so," the Marquis said. "We have been ordered to dock at Cologne."

"She will be . . . waiting for . . . me!" Daniela cried. "She will . . . take me . . . away with her . . . save me . . . oh, please . . . save me!"

"That is exactly what I am going to do," the Marquis answered.

He admired the effort with which she controlled the words that were trembling on her lips.

Then she asked in a frightened little voice:

"H-how can you . . . do that?"

"Very easily," the Marquis replied. "I want you to get out of bed."

"Yes . . . of course," Daniela said.

As she began to do so, he went to the wardrobe and opened the door.

Her gowns were hanging as Bowles had arranged them.

The Marquis looked at them for a moment, then he pressed something which Daniela could not see at the very top of the cupboard.

There was a faint "click" and the back of the cupboard slid away, showing a long, narrow aperture.

The Marquis pressed something else and the whole of the front of the wardrobe moved back until all the gowns had disappeared.

Then the back of the cupboard slid into place.

There was just an emptiness except for a belt which had fallen from one of the gowns and lay on the floor.

Daniela was watching open-mouthed.

"Bowles will see to everything else," he said. "Now come with me."

He was smiling as he spoke, knowing that what had just happened had seemed magical.

He thought it was something she would have expected of him.

Then he was aware that as he had told her to get out of bed, she had obeyed him.

She was standing in the cabin with the sunshine on her, and wearing only her nightgown.

He thought how very alluring it was and certainly proclaimed her innocence if he had ever doubted it.

He picked up the pretty silk negligée that was lying on a chair and helped her into it.

"Come," he said, "and I will bring one of your pillows so that you will be more comfortable."

She looked at him wide-eyed.

He was aware that she was very frightened, at the same time behaving exactly as he had expected her to do.

He took her into his own cabin, where he opened the wardrobe in which were hanging his own clothes.

Once again there was a "click" at the very top of it, and the back of the wardrobe slid to one side.

There was a dark aperture which Daniela thought was much deeper than the one in her cabin.

There was no need for the Marquis to tell her that was where she had to hide.

She slipped into it without his saying anything.

As she did so, he said very quietly:

"It will be dark, but there is plenty of air, and you will not suffocate. Keep very quiet, and I will let you out as soon as it is possible to do so."

He handed her the pillow as he was speaking, and she put it down on the floor and sat on it.

Then for a moment she looked up into the Marquis's eyes before he shut the back of the wardrobe.

He had, and it was something few people knew about him, been instrumental on several occasions in helping the Secretary of State for Foreign Affairs.

At different times he had smuggled Englishmen who were in trouble out of countries in which they had been unlawfully detained.

There had never been a whisper of his exploits among the gossips in London.

No one would have credited for a moment that the Marquis of Crowle could be involved in anything so dangerous, or in some cases diplomatically reprehensible.

It had been extremely difficult to smuggle people away without having a safe place for them to hide.

Therefore, when the Marquis had redecorated and added his new gadgets to the *Sea Horse* he had also contrived, under the greatest secrecy in the Shipyard, these two hiding places.

They would, he knew, hood-wink the Police of any country who were empowered to search the yacht.

He dressed quickly.

He was thinking that this was the first time that his "hidey-holes," as he called them, had been used by a woman.

When he was ready except for his tie and his yachting-jacket, he told Bowles to dispose of the rest of Daniela's clothes.

He had deliberately shown her what was happening so that she would not be frightened when she had to hide in the dark in the larger of the two places.

"Be careful you do not leave any trace of her to be seen, Bowles," the Marquis warned.

"Leave it ter me, M'Lord," Bowles replied.

The Marquis knew from the way the little man spoke he was enjoying every moment of the excitement.

Also, he liked being what he thought of as "one up" on the Police.

As Bowles disappeared into Daniela's cabin the Marquis went slowly and with dignity up to the Saloon.

The member of the River Police was just finishing a hearty breakfast and rose to his feet when the Marquis entered.

They shook hands, then the Marquis asked:

"Now, tell me what all this is about. I assure you my papers are in order, and my Captain had no trouble on his way to Baden-Baden."

"That is true," the Policeman replied, "but I understand that a charge has been brought against Your Excellency that you have kidnapped a minor."

The Marquis looked at him as if he did not understand what he was saying.

Then he exclaimed:

"I have never heard anything so ridiculous! This must be a joke, although I do not find it very funny!"

The Policeman looked uncomfortable.

The Marquis realised that at that moment they were turning into the harbour of Cologne.

The Captain then brought the *Sea Horse* into the part of the dock they had been allotted.

The *Kommissar*, a Senior Police Officer, very pompous

and important in his elaborate uniform, came aboard with two other Policemen.

He was, however, obviously impressed by the Marquis and the *Sea Horse*.

When he was brought into the Saloon by two stewards in their spotless uniforms he was, the Marquis was aware, more polite than he might otherwise have been in the circumstances.

He repeated what the Marquis had already been told.

After they had shaken hands, the Marquis sat down very much at his ease to listen to what the *Kommissar* had to tell him.

Then he said:

"As I have already said to the Officer who came aboard, I can only imagine this is some extraordinary joke. However if you are taking it seriously, *Mein Herr*, then of course I must send for the British Consul and ask him to protest at what is no less than an intrusion into my privacy!"

He spoke in such an authoritative manner that the *Kommissar* was obviously somewhat taken aback.

There was an uncomfortable pause until he said slowly:

"I have no wish, Your Excellency, to make this a Diplomatic incident."

"You are not going to suggest it is a criminal one?"

"No, no, certainly not!" the Officer replied. "Of course, the Lady who has brought the charge against you may have been mistaken."

"It is not a question of 'may,' " the Marquis said sharply, "she *is* mistaken, and I can only hope you will receive an apology for wasting your time, as I am certainly wasting mine!"

He hesitated a moment before he said:

"I do not want this talked about, *Mein Herr*, but I have

to return to England with the utmost speed, as my presence is required by Her Majesty Queen Victoria at Windsor Castle. You will therefore understand that in the circumstances, I have no wish to remain in Cologne for longer than is absolutely necessary."

The *Kommissar* was obviously deeply impressed.

"I can understand your feelings, Your Excellency," he said. "I suggest that if you would allow my men to search the yacht, I would then be in a position to report that the charge against you is unfounded."

The Marquis did not answer for a moment, as if he were thinking over what had been said.

Then he replied:

"Of course you are at liberty to inspect my yacht, and I can assure you, if you find what you are seeking, I shall be extremely surprised! On the other hand, if you do not, as I have already said, I think we are both within our rights to demand an apology."

"Then you agree, Your Excellency?" the *Kommissar* asked.

"Go ahead!" the Marquis replied in a lofty way. "My personal Valet will show your men every cabin and unlock the doors of those not in use."

The *Kommissar* gave an order.

The two men who were with him followed Bowles as he took them down the companionway.

"And now," the Marquis said, "I think you and I, *Mein Herr*, should have a glass of wine. It may be early in the morning, but these ridiculous incidents which I appreciate arise continually in both our lives, at least need not leave us thirsty!"

The *Kommissar* laughed and had actually drunk several

glasses of an excellent Hock before Bowles and the two Policemen returned.

The Marquis had taken only a small sip from his glass.

As the two Policemen came into the Saloon, only those who knew him very well would have been aware there was a slight tension in the way he turned his face towards them.

There was no need for either of the Policemen to speak.

They merely shook their heads and their Chief rose to his feet.

"I can only deeply regret, Your Excellency," he said politely, "that you have been disturbed and delayed by a charge which had no substance in fact. I shall make out a report to Headquarters, and I am sure you will receive a communiqué from them in due course."

The Marquis inclined his head.

Then, as the *Kommissar* clicked his heels together and bowed politely, he rose slowly from his chair.

"I am only glad, *Mein Herr*," he said, "that I can talk to Her Majesty of the beauty of your country, and the excellent attention I have received during the whole of my visit."

"I hope Your Excellency will visit us on another occasion," the *Kommissar* replied.

"I shall certainly consider it," the Marquis answered.

There was more bowing and clicking of heels and the Police left the Saloon.

The Marquis could only be thankful that the *Sea Horse* could now be once again on her way to England.

He was, however, too experienced to do anything too quickly.

He felt quite sure he was being watched.

He therefore went out on deck and stood where anyone watching from the shore could see him.

Soon they had left Cologne.

Only when he could no longer see the tower of the Cathedral, and on either side of him now were the magical cliffs and Castles that Daniela loved, did he go below.

He shut his cabin door, and because it was hot pulled off his yachting-jacket.

Then he manipulated the spring that opened the door to the secret hiding-place.

For a moment all he could see was darkness, and nothing moved inside.

"Daniela!" he said softly.

It was then she came out, not slowly or hesitatingly, but swiftly.

She was like a child coming from a dark place into the light and she flung herself against him, holding on to him frantically.

"You have . . . saved me . . . you have . . . saved . . . me!" she cried. "I heard their voices . . . and I was . . . frightened . . . terribly frightened . . . but now . . . once again . . . I am safe . . . with you!"

Then as if the tension and fear she had felt in the darkness overcame her, she burst into tears.

The Marquis's arms went round her as she cried helplessly.

He could feel the softness of her body trembling against his.

"It is all right," he said gently, "they have gone, they have apologised for suspecting me, and once again we have defeated your stepmother!"

"She . . . she will . . . try again . . . and again and . . . again!" Daniela cried. "What . . . can I . . . do? Where . . . can I . . . go?"

There was no answer to this.

134

The Marquis merely held her close, feeling that the strength of his arms and the fact that he was there were more comforting than words.

Finally she lifted her face and said a little incoherently:

"I . . . have . . . made you . . . w-wet!"

She had cried against his white linen shirt and he could feel it damp on his skin.

"It is not important," he said, "and I want you to smile. I expect, too, that you want your breakfast, as I want mine!"

Daniela gave a little chuckle.

"How can . . . you think of . . . breakfast," she asked, "when once again, with . . . your Shining Sword . . . which is your . . . clever mind, you have . . . defeated . . . the enemy?"

The Marquis thought as she looked up at him that with the tears on her cheeks, her shining eyes, and her smiling lips, nothing could be more lovely.

Then, as if he could not help himself, he bent his head and kissed her.

It was something he had not meant to do, but he had ceased to think or to reason.

What he was feeling at the moment for Daniela could be expressed only in kisses.

As he kissed her he felt her stiffen with surprise.

Then he found, as he had expected, that her lips were very soft beneath his, very young, and very innocent.

He knew that never in his whole life had he felt as he was feeling now.

It was very different from what he experienced when he kissed a woman with fiery passion because he desired her.

He had kissed Daniela because she was a child who had been frightened and whom he must protect and comfort.

Yet, as he felt the blood throbbing in his temples, it was as though he had suddenly come alive.

What he felt was nothing to do with her being a child, but very much a woman.

It was impossible not to draw her closer still.

Now, as his kisses became more demanding, more possessive, he was aware that she was feeling the same way as he was.

For her, however, it was an ecstasy which was carrying her, as she had told him before, up to the sky.

He was aware of her thoughts, her feelings, and the rapture that emanated from her.

He felt as if he, too, had stepped into the enchanted world in which Daniela believed.

He had always doubted it was there, but now he knew it was real.

In fact, it was more real than the world in which he lived, and which had always bored him.

Finally he raised his head, and he thought as he looked down at Daniela that she was transfigured.

She was so incredibly beautiful that he could only feel as if he were dreaming.

Her eyes shone, then, as if the wonder of him were too much for her, she hid her face against his neck.

In a very small voice that seemed to come from far away she asked:

"Is . . . is this . . . love?"

"It is love, my darling," the Marquis answered, "and I never believed that I should find it so unexpectedly, except that you are the most beautiful person I have ever seen, and I must never lose you!"

He felt her whole body quiver and knew it was not with fear.

"Now I... know I am... dreaming!" Daniela whispered. "Or... perhaps I... have died and... we are both... in Heaven!"

"We are alive," the Marquis said.

Then he was kissing her again, kissing her until he was quite sure they had reached the sky.

They were part of the prayer of thankfulness that Daniela had sent to God.

chapter seven

"Tomorrow we will be in Rotterdam," the Marquis remarked.

Daniela looked up at him apprehensively.

He knew she was thinking that perhaps the Police would come aboard again at the instigation of her stepmother.

The Marquis put his arm around her.

"You are not to be frightened, my precious," he said, "and I have a plan to which I hope you will agree."

"I will do . . . anything you . . . want," Daniela replied, "but I cannot help being a . . . little afraid . . . even when . . . I am with . . . you."

The Marquis pulled her closer, as if he were protecting her, then said:

"When we reach Rotterdam, we shall be out of Germany and into Holland, and therefore there will be no need for you to go on hiding."

He had been afraid that the Police, after being hood-winked at Cologne, might nevertheless still be watching the *Sea Horse*.

Therefore, as they moved down the Rhine, he had not allowed Daniela to go on deck until it was too dark for any watcher to be able to see her.

She sat with him in the Saloon or, which he thought was wiser, spent quite a considerable time in her cabin.

It was frustrating for both of them, but the Marquis was determined to take no chances.

He knew there was nothing more dangerous than a revengeful, evil woman like Esmé.

She would fight like a tiger to get hold of the money to which she had schemed to be entitled.

Daniela was so happy because the Marquis loved her that as long as they were with each other she thought it did not matter where they were.

She would be happy if they had to sit below in the Engine-Room or even in the dark cupboard in the Marquis's cabin.

At the same time, because she was so closely attuned to him, she knew, although he tried to conceal it from her, that he was anxious, and she felt the same.

She knew even better than the Marquis how determined her stepmother was. How her beloved father had suffered at her hands!

"She would . . . kill me," she told herself in the quietness of the night, "rather than . . . let me be . . . happy."

Then she thought she would not even mind dying herself if it prevented her stepmother from injuring the Marquis.

She was so entirely unprincipled that Daniela was quite sure she would never forgive the Marquis for interrupting the Marriage Service and spiriting her away out of her grasp.

Daniela tossed and turned and found it impossible to sleep.

She thought her stepmother would not easily accept the Police report that there was no woman on board with the Marquis.

Being a woman, she would suspect that he had concealed her somewhere.

Every time they passed a Town, Daniela was afraid that the Police would come aboard again.

If they did, they would be more thorough in their search than they had been at Cologne.

However, they had reached the end of the Rhine.

As the Marquis had said, tomorrow they would be in Holland.

Daniela knew very little about Holland.

At School the teachers had always made it sound rather dull and unexciting.

But as she stood on deck with the Marquis, and the *Sea Horse* moved as swiftly through the darkness as it had through the daylight, it was for the moment a Golden Land.

It was, she knew, the Gateway to the North Sea, and after that they would be home.

As if the Marquis knew what she was thinking, he said quietly:

"Do you want to hear my plan, my precious one?"

"Of course I . . . do," Daniela answered. "You know I love . . . your plans. You are so clever . . . so brilliant . . . and no one else would think in the same way as you do."

The Marquis knew that was the way he wanted Daniela to think about him.

At the same time, for him it was a new experience that a woman should praise his mind rather than his body.

Then he told himself that in every way Daniela was different from anybody he had ever known before.

Every moment he was with her he felt himself falling more and more in love.

It was extraordinary that he had to wait until he was as old as he was now before he realised the depth, height, and strength of being in love.

He knew that what he had thought of before as love was really lust, an entirely physical desire which could burn fiercely for a short time.

However, it died away until there was not even a glowing ember left to make him remember what he had once felt.

What he felt for Daniela was progressive.

Every day he found new aspects of her character and personality which enthralled him.

He found himself lying awake at night, thinking over things she had said.

He realised it was because she was so unselfconscious, so natural, that they were words of wisdom. They came from her heart and her soul and owed nothing to artifice.

Now he could just see her looking up at him in the light from the stars.

He told himself that once they were clear of the danger that menaced them from Esmé Blanc, they would grow together in nobility and understanding which would benefit not only themselves.

In time it would benefit their children and everybody with whom they came in contact.

It was these thoughts that brought back to him the ideals of chivalry he had as a very young man.

These had soon been swept away by life in the Social World, by the promiscuous behaviour of the beautiful women with whom he had spent his time and the cynical attitude of the men who pursued them.

To them a lovely woman was fair game.

But the Marquis knew, although he would not admit it to himself, that what he really wanted to find in his life was a woman he could not only love but worship.

He wanted to worship her purity, because she was intrinsically good, both in thought and in deed.

This was what he had found in Daniela.

He told himself a hundred times a day that he was the luckiest man in the world.

Now, as he looked down at her, he knew, too, that she was more beautiful than anybody he had ever seen.

It was not only because of her features, her hair, or the clearness of her skin.

It was because her beauty came from within and radiated, he thought, like a Divine Light.

He realised she was waiting for him to speak, and after a moment he said:

"My plan is, my precious, that before we return to England and face what I know will be a number of problems, we should be married."

He saw Daniela's eyes widen, and she moved a little closer to him, as if she wanted to be sure he was there.

"Married?" she whispered. "Is that . . . possible?"

"I know you may feel that things are moving too quickly," he said, "since your father died such a short time ago, but I have been thinking that even in England, unless you are with me both by day and by night, it will be difficult for me to protect you and make sure you are safe."

Daniela knew he was thinking of her stepmother.

Impulsively she put out her hand to hold on to him.

"Please . . . please," she said, "I . . . I want to be . . . with you! I shall be . . . very frightened if I am . . . alone and . . . you are not . . . there."

"I should be afraid too," the Marquis said in his deep voice. "If I lost you now, my darling, I should have lost everything that matters to me in life."

"Do you . . . mean that . . . do you . . . really mean . . . it?" Daniela asked.

"I love you so overwhelmingly," the Marquis said, "that I cannot put it into words. It is something I will be able to express better, and very much more eloquently, once you are my wife."

"Then please . . . let us be . . . married," Daniela pleaded, "although I am . . . afraid people . . . may be . . . shocked."

She thought he did not understand and added:

"I am not . . . thinking of myself . . . I am not important . . . but you are of . . . such consequence . . . and Queen Victoria might be . . . angry with you!"

"I am not concerned with Her Majesty or anyone except you," the Marquis said. "The only thing that matters, my precious little love, is that you should be married to me so that I can fight your battles as you want me to do."

She smiled.

He knew she was thinking of him once again as a Knight in Shining Armour.

He was setting out to destroy the Dragon or any enemy which frightened her.

"When we reach Rotterdam," the Marquis said, "I am going to tell the Captain to dock in the harbour and we will go to the British Consulate."

There was a pause, then Daniela asked.

"Did . . . you say . . . 'we'? You are . . . not going to . . . leave me aboard the . . . *Sea Horse*?"

"No, of course not," the Marquis replied. "We will go together. I am certain once we are there I can make the arrangements I want, especially as I happen to know the Consul personally."

Daniela hid her face against his shoulder.

"You . . . are quite . . . certain," she said in a very low voice, "that you will . . . never regret . . . marrying me?"

The Marquis's arms tightened and she went on:

"I . . . I know your family would . . . expect you to have a . . . very grand wedding at . . . St. George's in Hanover Square, with the . . . Prince of Wales . . . there and . . . all your other . . . important friends."

"I am telling you the truth," the Marquis answered, "when I say that I would much rather be married very quietly with no one in the Church but us."

"That is . . . what I would . . . like too," Daniela said. "But we will not be . . . alone because . . . Mama and Papa will be . . . watching over us . . . and I know that . . . God will bless us . . . as He has . . . already in . . . letting us . . . find each other."

"That is exactly what I want," the Marquis said, and it was the truth.

* * *

The *Sea Horse* reached Rotterdam early in the morning and docked when the Port was just beginning to be busy.

Because the Marquis was half-afraid the River Police might come aboard as they had at Cologne, he ordered Daniela's breakfast to be taken to her cabin.

He ate in the Saloon.

A seaman was sent ashore to find the nearest Livery Stable and procure a comfortable carriage preferably drawn by two horses.

As the sun rose over the Town the Marquis took Daniela

down the gangplank to where the carriage was waiting.

As he had ordered, there was a coachman and a footman on the box, and the carriage was a very comfortable one.

He thought it must have once belonged to a nobleman before it had ended up in the Livery Stable.

The horses set off.

As Daniela slipped her hand into his, the Marquis thought she was looking particularly lovely.

She was wearing one of the very expensive white gowns her stepmother had insisted on her buying in Paris.

With it was an attractive bonnet trimmed with white flowers.

She looked like a flower herself, he thought.

He knew that while he had encountered many lovely women in his life, Daniela was by far the loveliest, and the most precious.

He felt her fingers quiver in his and he asked:

"You are not frightened, my darling?"

"A little," she answered, "but so far . . . there are no Police . . . and no one . . . threatening us."

Her voice quivered on the last two words.

The Marquis raised her hand to his lips and kissed her fingers, one after the other.

"You have to trust me," he said, "and I swear to you that no one shall take you from me! Once you are my wife, it will be impossible for anyone to do so."

Daniela's smile was part of the sunshine as they drove on in silence.

The British Consulate was, the Marquis thought, exactly like every British Consulate in every part of the world.

It was an imposing white building with the Union Jack flying from a flagstaff outside.

Sentries were standing outside their boxes on either side of the porticoed front door.

Through the wrought-iron gateway there was a formal garden with flower-beds planted with red geraniums surrounded by blue and white lobelia.

They stepped out of the carriage and the Marquis asked to see the Consul, Sir Robert Fraser Turing.

After a short wait in an ante-room they were taken to the Consul's private Study.

A tall, elegant man rose when they were announced and held out his hand.

"My dear Crowle!" he exclaimed in surprise. "You are the last person I expected to see in Holland."

"I can only say I am delighted to find you here," the Marquis replied, "because I need your help."

He introduced Daniela and was aware that Sir Robert looked at her with surprise and at the same time with undoubted admiration.

Sir Robert invited them to sit down and then asked:

"What can I do for you? I have followed your success in the racing world, and must congratulate you on winning last year the Gold Cup at Ascot."

"I was fortunate," the Marquis said, "but I have no time to talk to you about horses now. There is something very much more serious."

He paused for a moment. Then he said:

"As I think, Sir Robert, that what I have to tell you will upset Miss Brooke, I wonder if it would be possible for her to talk to your wife for a few minutes? Or, alternatively, to be with some member of your staff whom you trust, for I do not wish her to be alone."

Now there was no doubt of the surprise in Sir Robert's eyes as he said:

"Of course! My wife will be delighted, and she is in the Drawing-Room at the moment, writing letters to our children in England."

"Well, I am sure Miss Brooke will be safe with her!" the Marquis smiled.

Sir Robert rose to his feet.

As he did so, Daniela gave the Marquis a nervous glance which told him she did not wish to leave him.

"I will not be long," he said quietly.

She therefore followed Sir Robert across the room and he took her into the Drawing-Room, where Lady Fraser Turing suggested they should have a cup of coffee together.

She was a charming person who had been very pretty when she was young.

There was a kindness about her which reminded Daniela of her mother.

Sir Robert returned to his Study.

"Now, what is all this about, Crowle?" he asked. "As you can imagine, I am consumed with curiosity!"

The Marquis told him the whole story:

How Esmé Blanc had drugged Lord Seabrooke to marry him, and had been instrumental in causing his death in a duel.

He explained how having discovered she had been left very little money in Lord Seabrooke's Will she had tried to marry Daniela off to her lover, who he suspected would then be a Bigamist.

He told him how the River Police had searched his yacht for Daniela at Cologne.

As he finished speaking, Sir Robert literally gasped at him.

"If I did not know you were a truthful man," he said,

"I would think I was listening to the plot of a sensational novel, or a drama from a Play House."

"I thought you would feel like that," the Marquis said. "But you will understand, Sir Robert, we are being menaced by this woman, and it is therefore important, as Daniela and I have fallen in love, that we should be married immediately!"

"Immediately?" Sir Robert exclaimed.

"That is the right word," the Marquis said, "and I imagine in Rotterdam there is a Protestant Church available and a Parson of our own faith?"

"Yes, of course," Sir Robert agreed. "You can be married at the Church which practically adjoins this building and where I and my staff worship. We have an English Parson who officiates at every official occasion."

The Marquis smiled.

"That is exactly what I expected."

"All the formalities for the marriage," Sir Robert went on, "can be arranged here in my office, and I have only to send for the Parson to tell him what is required."

"Then I would be very obliged," the Marquis said, "if you would do that at once."

He smiled before continuing:

"I may seem unduly anxious, but I have a feeling that the new Lady Seabrooke will realise that by this time we have left Germany and she will either try to make trouble in Rotterdam, or else wait until we reach England."

"Can nothing be done about an appalling woman like that?"

"To prove her crime in the French Courts would be very difficult," the Marquis said slowly. "I fear that her marriage to Lord Seabrooke would be held to be legal. Though he claimed he had no memory of the Service taking place, he is no longer alive to say so."

Sir Robert made a sound of despair.

"If Miss Brooke had actually been married to *Comte* André de Sauzan, I am sure it would be possible to prove Bigamy. But that would not involve Lady Seabrooke, who would, of course, deny all knowledge of it."

"You are right," Sir Robert said, "but women like that should be exterminated!"

"I agree with you," the Marquis said, "but the question is—how? And I cannot have her upsetting my future wife any further than she has done already."

"It must have been a terrible ordeal for the poor girl," Sir Robert said sympathetically. "By the way, I have not yet congratulated you! I have never seen anyone more lovely! She is just like her mother."

He paused as if he were thinking before he went on:

"I remember seeing Lady Seabrooke at Buckingham Palace and thinking that without exception she was the most beautiful woman in the Throne Room."

"That is what my wife will be in the future," the Marquis said quietly.

Sir Robert called his private secretary to give him a number of instructions, then took the Marquis into the Drawing-Room to meet his wife.

Lady Fraser Turing, when she heard that the Marquis was to be married, looked at him a little archly.

"I have always understood, My Lord, that you were a sworn bachelor, but I can understand your change of heart when you meet anyone so lovely as Miss Brooke."

The Marquis saw Daniela blush at the compliment.

He thought the colour in her cheeks and her shyness was very appealing.

For a moment they looked at each other and everything else was forgotten.

Then the Marquis said to Lady Turing:

"Your husband has been kind enough to arrange for our marriage to take place immediately, but I have one more favour to ask. Would it be possible for you to lend us a wedding-ring, or, alternatively, perhaps we could send to the nearest Jeweller?"

Sir Robert laughed.

"It is unlike you, Crowle, not to be prepared for any emergency! But I expect my wife can oblige."

"Actually I can," Lady Fraser Turing said. "I have my mother's wedding-ring, and I am sure it will fit Miss Brooke."

"Are you sure you do not mind parting with it?" Daniela asked in a low voice. "You may think it strange that I do not have my own mother's, but Mama was so happy in her marriage to my father that she left a letter saying if she died, she wanted to be buried wearing her wedding-ring."

She smiled before the went on:

"She also wanted to wear a necklace which was the first present my father ever gave her."

"I can understand that," Lady Fraser Turing said softly, "and it is something I shall want myself if I die before my husband."

Sir Robert held up his hands and exclaimed:

"We must not have all this talk of death! We are celebrating His Lordship's wedding! I am going to open a bottle of champagne so that we can all have a drink and wish the bride and bridegroom every possible happiness and a very long life together."

"Of course we must do that," his wife agreed, "and I think, while the champagne's coming, I will take Miss

Brooke upstairs. I expect she would like to tidy herself before we go to the Church.''

Upstairs in a very pretty bedroom with windows overlooking an attractive garden at the back of the house, Lady Fraser Turing said:

''I have always been a great admirer, as my husband is, of your future husband. He is a very clever man, and Lord Stanley, the Secretary of State for Foreign Affairs, has a great respect for him.''

''He is very . . . very . . . clever,'' Daniela replied, ''and I am rather afraid he may find me . . . boring.''

Lady Fraser Turing smiled.

''I think that is very unlikely! I have spent so much of my time in diplomatic circles that I have learnt to recognise a man's true feelings, which are often very different from what he says!''

She smiled again before she went on:

''When the Marquis came into the room I saw the way he looked at you. I promise you it would be impossible for any mere actor, however clever, to look as he did, which was very, very much in love!''

''And I love him . . . with all my heart,'' Daniela said, ''and will try to . . . make him a . . . good wife.''

Lady Fraser Turing bent and kissed her.

''You are exactly the wife he should have,'' she said. ''He is a very lucky man!''

When Daniela went downstairs and accepted the glass of champagne which Sir Robert gave her, she hoped the Marquis thought she looked pretty enough to be his bride.

Because she could not help herself, she went to his side and slipped her hand into his.

She knew as his fingers tightened on hers that he was telling her how much he loved her, and how once they were married there would be no more problems, and no need for her to be afraid.

She had been in the Drawing-Room for only a few minutes when the door opened and Sir Robert's private secretary said:

"I have been asked to tell you, Sir, that the Chaplain is waiting in the Church."

Daniela expected that the Consul and his wife would accompany them.

But as she and the Marquis followed the secretary who led them to a side door of the Consulate, she found they were alone.

A footman, however, when they emerged from the Drawing-Room, had handed the Marquis a bouquet of white roses and lilies-of-the-valley.

He gave it to Daniela.

She knew that it must have been fetched from a shop in the Town while they were in the Consulate.

It was only a short walk through the garden to the Church that was just outside.

As she was walking beside the Marquis and holding his hand, Daniela felt as if the sun were more brilliant than she had ever known it before.

She could hear the birds singing in the trees, saw the bees and the butterflies hovering about the flowers.

The fragrance from them seemed more intense because she was so happy.

The Church was old and had an atmosphere that made her feel that the spirits of many generations of people who had worshipped there were still around them.

She remembered her father once saying: "Holland is the great Protestant Fortress of Western Europe."

The sun shone through the beautiful ancient stained glass windows.

Holding on to the Marquis's arm, she moved with him slowly up the aisle.

The organ was playing very softly and the Clergyman, an elderly man, read the words of the Marriage Service with an unmistakable sincerity.

To Daniela it was a moment of rapture that was part of her love for the Marquis.

She was certain, as she had told him, that her father and mother were there, happy because she had found a man who loved her for herself, and whom she loved with every breath she drew.

Then the ring was on her finger and they knelt for the Blessing.

She was sure that the music came not from the organ but from Heaven.

'I belong to him . . . I am his wife and . . . I am safe for ever!' Daniela thought.

Then she was saying over and over again in her heart:

"Thank You, God, thank You!"

She walked down the aisle, again on the Marquis's arm.

He took her to the West Door and not to the side door through which they had entered the Church.

She realised that he had anticipated her wishes without her having to voice them.

She felt it would somehow spoil the wonder of the Service and the rapture she had felt during it if they had to go back to the Consulate and be polite.

It was so like the Marquis, she thought, to know exactly what she would want to make their happiness even more marvellous than it was already.

As they stopped at the top of the steps in the sunshine, she gave him a radiant smile.

Then he helped her into their carriage.

She knew they were going straight back to the yacht.

They drove away and the horses began to gather pace down the broad street which ran past the front of the Consulate building.

The Marquis, looking into Daniela's eyes, had no idea that coming towards them was an open carriage drawn by one horse and containing Esmé Seabrooke.

When she saw a carriage coming apparently from the Consulate, which she had been told at the Livery Stable had been hired by the Marquis, she shouted at her own coachman to stop.

As he obeyed her orders, Esmé Seabrooke opened her carriage-door and sprang out.

She ran across the road, waving her arms.

By this time the Marquis's carriage was almost past her.

His coachmen, who were talking together, were unaware of her approach.

Furiously she screamed at the occupants inside the carriage, gesticulating at them as she did so.

But the Marquis had put his arms round Daniela and was kissing her with long, slow, passionate kisses.

They were lost to the world outside.

Esmé Seabrooke turned away, but the wheel of the carriage touched her ankle and threw her down onto the road.

She fell in front of a van being driven in haste by a young man who had little control over his horses.

Esmé was directly in their path, and one of the horses rearing in fright struck her in the face.

Before the driver had any idea of what was happening, the wheels of the van had passed over her.

She was taken to Hospital, but died before she arrived there.

It was more than seven days before the information reached the British Consulate that a woman by the name of Lady Seabrooke was lying in the mortuary.

The news was then transmitted to the Marquis and the Marchioness of Crowle in England.

*   *   *

When they arrived back at the *Sea Horse* luncheon was waiting for them.

Having no idea there was now no hurry for them to leave Rotterdam, the Marquis gave the order to cast off immediately and proceed on their voyage to England.

Now Daniela could go out on deck in the sunshine, and it did not matter if she was seen.

But all she wanted to do was to look at the Marquis.

The Chef had surpassed himself in his efforts to make their Wedding-Breakfast memorable.

Yet they had little idea of what they were eating.

To Daniela it was simply the ambrosia of the gods.

When the meal was finished and the Marquis suggested they should go below, she agreed eagerly.

She thought he intended to kiss her, but when they reached her cabin he said:

"I think, my darling, as you were up so early, and so was I, we should rest, and as it is very hot on deck, it will be cooler in your cabin."

Daniela looked at him enquiringly, not quite certain what he meant.

He pulled her against him and said:

"I want you close to me, my precious, and now that you are my wife, I will teach you about love! It will be the most exciting thing I have ever done in my whole life!"

He kissed her gently.

She went into her cabin and undressed quickly. She put on the prettiest nightgown she had before she got into bed.

Then she was half-afraid she had mistaken the Marquis's intentions.

He might think it very strange of her to be going to bed in the middle of the day, when he came into her cabin.

Now she saw that he, too, had undressed and was wearing a long silk robe, and she knew her fears were unfounded.

He sat down on the bed close to her and, taking her hand, he said:

"How is it possible that anyone can look so beautiful?"

As he felt her fingers quiver in his he asked:

"You are not frightened of me, my precious little wife?"

"N-not of . . . you," she answered. "But . . . suppose after all you have said . . . I disappoint you?"

The Marquis smiled.

"That is impossible!"

"Why?"

"Because you are exactly what I have been looking for all my life, but did not realise it."

He smiled at her lovingly before continuing:

"I had made up my mind not to marry simply because I thought any woman would bore me after a short while. And yet, deep in my heart, I believed that one day I would find— you."

"That is . . . a wonderful thing for . . . you to say to me," Daniela whispered, "but . . . will you promise me something?"

"I will promise you anything you ask me," the Marquis replied.

"Will you . . . promise that if I do . . . anything wrong . . .

157

you will tell me? If I make . . . mistakes you will not be . . . angry?''

''I promise,'' the Marquis said.

''And please . . . please . . . my wonderful . . . clever husband . . . teach me to be . . . exactly as you want me to be.''

The Marquis thought no one could speak so movingly, but although his lips were aching for hers, he did not kiss her.

Instead, he took off his robe and got into bed beside her.

He pulled her against him.

Then, as he touched her, he was aware that she was swept by her love into a magical world which was part of Fairyland and part, too, of Heaven.

And he kissed her possessively, demandingly, and at the same time tenderly.

It was a kiss that expressed his love.

He knew that he had found a perfection that was Divine and Daniela had found the same.

She was so beautiful that she had become a part of his soul, while for her he was part of the beauty that she found everywhere and in life itself.

He drew her closer and closer still, and his kisses became more demanding and more passionate.

He also felt the blessing they had received in the Church.

He thought that the God who had brought them together had enveloped them with a light.

It was so brilliant that it could only have come from Him, yet it also came from themselves.

It was the ecstasy of love, the rapture and wonder for which all men seek.

''I love you!'' Daniela was saying. ''I . . . love you . . . and I can . . . hear the . . . music in . . . the air . . . which is also . . . singing in my . . . heart!''

"As it is singing in mine!" the Marquis said. "My beautiful darling, I love you, and now you are safe for ever and I will protect you and worship you until the world comes to an end."

"I shall . . . always feel . . . safe with you," Daniela said, "but love me . . . please . . . love me!"

The music seemed to swell to a crescendo of glory, and the light within them was blinding.

They were no longer on earth, but in a Heaven of their own.

There was no fear, no evil, but only Love.

ABOUT THE AUTHOR

Barbara Cartland, the world's most famous romantic novelist, who is also an historian, playwright, lecturer, political speaker and television personality, has now written over 507 books and sold nearly 500 million copies all over the world.

She has also had many historical works published and has written four autobiographies as well as the biographies of her mother and that of her brother, Ronald Cartland, who was the first Member of Parliament to be killed in the last war. This book has a preface by Sir Winston Churchill and has just been republished with an introduction by Sir Arthur Bryant.

Love at the Helm, a novel written with the help and inspiration of the late Earl Mountbatten of Burma, Great Uncle of His Royal Highness The Prince of Wales, is being sold for the Mountbatten Memorial Trust.

She has broken the world record for the last thirteen years by writing an average of twenty-three books a year. In the *Guinness Book of Records* she is listed as the world's top-selling author.

Miss Cartland in 1978 sang an Album of Love Songs with the Royal Philharmonic Orchestra.

In private life Barbara Cartland, who is a Dame of the Order of St. John of Jerusalem, Chairman of the St. John Council in Hertfordshire and Deputy President of the St.

John Ambulance Brigade, has fought for better condition and salaries for Midwives and Nurses.

She championed the cause for the Elderly in 1956 invoking a Government Enquiry into the "Housing Condition of Old People."

In 1962 she had the Law of England changed so th Local Authorities had to provide camps for their own Gypsies. This has meant that since then thousands and thousand of Gypsy children have been able to go to School, whic they had never been able to do in the past, as their caravan were moved every twenty-four hours by the Police.

There are now fourteen camps in Hertfordshire and Barbara Cartland has her own Romany Gypsy Camp calle Barbaraville by the Gypsies.

Her designs "Decorating with Love" are being sold a over the U.S.A. and the National Home Fashions Leagu made her, in 1981, "Woman of Achievement."

She is unique in that she was one and two in the Dalto list of Best Sellers, and one week had four books in the to twenty.

Barbara Cartland's book *Getting Older, Growir Younger* has been published in Great Britain and the U.S.A and her fifth cookery book, *The Romance of Food*, is no being used by the House of Commons.

In 1984 she received at Kennedy Airport America Bishop Wright Air Industry Award for her contribution the development of aviation. In 1931 she and two R.A.I Officers thought of, and carried, the first aeroplane-towe glider airmail.

During the War she was Chief Lady Welfare Officer Bedfordshire looking after 20,000 Service men and women She thought of having a pool of Wedding Dresses at th

War Office so a Service Bride could hire a gown for the day.

She bought 1,000 gowns without coupons for the A.T.S., the W.A.A.F's and the W.R.E.N.S. In 1945 Barbara Cartland received the Certificate of Merit from Eastern Command.

In 1964 Barbara Cartland founded the National Association for Health of which she is the President, as a front for all the Health Stores and for any product made as alternative medicine.

This is now a £500,000 turnover a year, with one third going in export.

In January 1988 she received *La Médaille de Vermeil de la Ville de Paris*. This is the highest award to be given in France by the City of Paris for achievement—25 million books sold in France.

In March 1988 Barbara Cartland was asked by the Indian Government to open their Health Resort outside Delhi. This is almost the largest Health Resort in the world.

Barbara Cartland was received with great enthusiasm by her fans, who fêted her at a reception in the City, and she received the gift of an embossed plate from the Government.